"Our Guy"
Or The Elder Brother

by

Mrs. E. E. Boyd

ISBN: 978-93-64280-07-5

Published by

DOUBLE 9 BOOKS

2/13-B, Ansari Road
Daryaganj, New Delhi – 110002
info@double9books.com
www.double9books.com
Tel. 011-40042856

ABOUT THE AUTHOR

Mrs. E. E. Boyd, the author of "Our Guy," was an early 20th-century writer known for her contributions to domestic fiction and social commentary. Her work often explores themes related to **family life, social issues,** and **character development**. Boyd's novels typically delve into the complexities of **family dynamics** and **community life,** reflecting on **societal expectations** and the emotional challenges faced by individuals. Her storytelling combines elements of **romantic drama** with a focus on **personal growth** and **conflict resolution**. Although, not as widely recognized today, Boyd's work provides valuable insights into the social and domestic issues of her time, offering readers a glimpse into early 20th-century perspectives on **moral values** and **character relationships.** Her narratives often highlight the interplay between personal desires and societal norms, making her contributions to literature both engaging and thought -provoking.

CONTENTS

CHAPTER I
NEW YEAR'S EVE

HE had gone, the good old year! It was no wonder people sighed as his pulse beat slower and slower, for he had brightened many hearts and gladdened many homes. If he had brought sadness and heart-ache to some, it was only that he never once failed in any duty. Taking from the hand that had given him life-joys and sorrows, hopes and disappointments, crosses and ease, he gave unto each one what the Master designed. But it happens very often that the rosy morning ends in a night dark and tempestuous, while the clouds that greet our early waking, are followed by the bright shining of the sun. And there is no life which would not be more bright and joyous, if it only opened the windows and let the light God means it to have, shine in.

So there were sighs and regrets as there always are, when one who has been true and kind, has left us forever.

Out on the frosty air floated the sound of bells. Merrily, joyously they pealed forth to welcome the new life that had just dawned, while from far and near the guns gave out their noisy greeting.

Sad hearts brightened, tearful faces smiled. With their old friend had gone the old life; they would throw aside regret and be brave and strong. Among an assembly of silent worshippers knelt two sisters side by side. It was as if they had gathered round the bedside of a departing one, trying to catch the last look and to hear the last sound, the stillness only broken by sobs from wrung hearts. Tremblingly their girlish voices united with the multitude, as with a covenant-keeping God they renewed their covenant in the words:—

"Come, let us use the grace divine,
And all with one accord,

In a perpetual cov'nant join
Ourselves to Christ the Lord;

Give up ourselves through Jesus' power
His name to glorify,
And promise in this sacred hour
For God to live and die.

The cov'nant we this moment make,
Be ever kept in mind;
We will no more our God forsake,
Or cast his words behind.

We never will throw off his fear,
Who hears our solemn vow,
And if thou art well pleased to hear,
Come down and meet us now.

Thee, Father, Son, and Holy Ghost,
Let all our hearts receive;
Present with the celestial host,
The peaceful answer give.

To each the cov'nant blood apply,
Which takes our sins away;
And register our names on high,
And keep us to that day."

At the words, "We will no more our God forsake," the voice of the eldest suddenly failed, and burying her face she sobbed aloud. The other seemed to have gathered strength with every word, and now as she sang:—

"We never will throw off his fear
Who hears our solemn vow;—"

her voice rang out clear and steady. To her sister it already had an air of triumph, and caused her to look up wonderingly into the face so full of trust and holy purpose. The clear, bright eyes met her tearful gaze; there was a pressure of the hand as entreatingly she said, "Sing, Ruth; the *Lord* is our strength, He will help us."

Re-assured and comforted, Ruth sang, "To each the cov'nant blood apply," thinking of her sister's words, and feeling already His help.

The New Year's hymn was sung, friends looked into each other's faces with words of cheer, and then separated. They went their ways to carry out their purposes, and with them went Ruth and Agnes.

The girls were orphans. For ten years they had been motherless, and several years previous their father had died. They had no one but their brother Guy, not even a distant relative, and this made them cling very closely to one another. One day when Guy was in a very gay and gracious mood, he took his sisters by the arm and whirling them round sang, "Lovers three are we, no truer could you see," to which Ruth laughingly added, "And we'll faithful be, Guy, Agnes and me."

But they were not demonstrative. That is they rarely kissed each other; they did not show their love in these many ways that are so beautiful among brothers and sisters. Somehow they had never learned them, for their father had been a stern, forbidding man, who would have called such things "Stuff, and Nonsense," and their mother was very timid, looking up to her husband in everything. She would not have dared to teach her children these endearing ways. Sometimes she said "dear," and kissed them, and O, how their hearts filled up with love! It made them happy for days after. But they always knew she loved them even more than words or caresses could express, and they gave her back the strength of their young, loving natures. When she left them they drew up closer to each other in thought, loving silently, yet with greater intensity.

Guy, the eldest, was twenty-two and Agnes eighteen. He had just been admitted to the bar, and expected to stand high in his profession before long. His sisters were sure if any one rose, he certainly would, for he had not only ambition but talent, and in speaking of "our Guy," they dwelt on the name with great tenderness and pride. He assured them that no one had made a higher mount at first than he, having rented a third story room, and as the girls did not know much about such matters they were quite satisfied.

Agnes was confiding, truthful. "Saintly," Guy called her. She did not know how to reason about things as Ruth, she said, and "of course was not so wise;" but withall she was stronger and wiser, for she had learned the true wisdom of leaving everything in the hands of God, knowing that He could better order them than she. And knowing this, she did not question His providences, although they were many times painful and hard to understand. He was to her always a loving Father, and she wanted to be to him a loving, dutiful child.

Ruth was intensely earnest and more practical than Agnes. She believed in the exercise of judgment and not such entire dependence upon the Lord; the latter kept one weak she thought, and she did not see the sense of doing anything that she could not quite understand. So in spiritual things she very often took her own way, but it did not satisfy; her life seemed a life of failure, while Agnes never appeared to be disappointed. They often talked to each other about these things and Ruth felt strange after their talks and more confident of success, but her unsanctified will, her efforts at self-government brought the same result as before.

Guy was not a Christian, he had not even gone much to church since he began to study law, but he was a good, kind brother, and the sisters were sure he would come out right some time. If they had given the reason of their assurance, Agnes would have said, she prayed for it and believed that God would answer prayer, while Ruth's reply would have been, "He is our Guy, and of course he will die a Christian." The girls did not talk so much to their brother as to each other; he could not understand their "spiritual talks," and his life and theirs were after all so different. But when he spent an evening at home as he occasionally did, their joy was extreme. Agnes then was sure the Lord meant to answer her prayer very soon, and asked to be directed so that she might draw her brother to Christ by her consistent life. Ruth exerted herself to the utmost to entertain him. Watching him very closely to see the effect of her efforts, and being rewarded by some such remark as: "Ruth, you are becoming quite brilliant; it will not do to have you cooped up here; you must see more of the world."

That satisfied her; she knew she was doing him good, and she would not stop at anything to accomplish her purpose. For while she was not so keenly alive to spiritual things as Agnes, she saw as Agnes never appeared to see, the danger there was of his being led astray, knowing how few real Christians were to be found in the legal professions.

The girls had had many struggles during the last few years, even since Guy commenced the study of law. And he had not been without his difficulties. It had been a hard fight between his love of profession and love for his sisters. So that many a time he resolved to throw aside his books and earn a livelihood in some other way, any way rather than have them helping him. But whenever he mentioned it, they seemed so distressed that he yielded the point, resolved to study with more earnestness so that one day they might be proud of him. He did not know already how proud they were, or what pleasure it was to make sacrifices for him; for they never hinted at the self-denial they were called upon continually to practice.

It had occurred to Guy's mind frequently that he ought to spend more time with his sisters, that being alone, their evenings must be dull; but home always suggested that which he wanted to drive from his thoughts as much as possible; hard toiling and sacrifice on the part of his sisters. If he kept this before him constantly, he reasoned, it would so dishearten and depress him that his chance of success would be naturally lessened. Indeed his spirits must be kept up or he give up altogether. When he began to make money, things should be very different; he would devote himself entirely to them. But with diplomas, fortunes do not come, and so it was rarely that the girls had their brother home with them. When they did, we have seen how it cheered and re-assured them.

On the death of their father it was ascertained that very little support was left for his family, and Guy entered a store at a very small salary, while Ruth was compelled to remain at home on account of her mother's delicate health. She managed to obtain a few scholars, however, and every month had a little to add to the general fund. Agnes, then too young to support herself or others, continued to go to school, and in time received a teacher's certificate. But as she was not yet old enough to obtain a situation in the public schools, she helped Ruth with hers which had increased in size, making quite a good appearance in the second story back room.

They were at that time living comfortably, when Guy, who had never liked the store, expressed his ardent desire to study law. He was rather surprised to find the readiness with which his mother consented, and the eagerness of his sisters. Speaking truthfully, they thought him far above his present business and much preferred that he should have a profession. So it was not long until he was in a lawyer's office. Then their mother died. It seemed a very cruel thing to Guy that she should be taken away just now; if she could only have lived a few years longer to see her son a great man; he had determined to repay her for all her devotion.

Ruth soon had to do without her assistant when Agnes, with a bright, cheerful heart, went out into the world "to help Guy and Ruth." And now the sisters are teaching, while "Guy Gorton, Attorney at Law," mounts his three flights of stairs daily, with a great deal of hope, and as large a share of importance.

CHAPTER II
DIFFERENTLY CONSTITUTED

NEITHER of the girls could tell which awoke first on New Year's morning, for as Agnes said at the breakfast table, when they looked at each other they were both awake.

Guy declared it was no wonder she graduated with such high honor when she was so extremely wise; and Ruth gave it as her opinion that she always had been a most precocious child, relating instances, some of them so amusing that with the recollection came a general outburst of merriment. "Do you remember the time the Millerites were making such an ado about the world coming to an end, Guy, how she went to mother and asked if it twisted itself round and round until it came to the end?"

"Don't I though, and the day she asked mother if *vertigo* meant a monkey. When mother told her no and laughed, she said it must be some animal, for she read in the paper that a man went up into a tree and while there was seized with vertigo."

"And the day she was transferred to another school, when she said she had a note of transubstantiation."

"Yes, and"—Guy was about to continue, but Agnes declared she was not going to sit there as a target for their fun, and ran laughing out of the room.

"What are you going to do with yourselves, girls?" asked their brother, as lighting a cigar he prepared to go out.

"O we are going to stay at home and have a nice time; you know holidays don't come very often."

"Well, you women folks have queer ideas of a nice time, if that is what you call staying in the house. Why, it is enough to make you stupid. Fix yourself up like other girls, and promenade; that is what I mean to do."

"What, fix yourself up like other girls?" demurely asked Agnes, glad of an opportunity to pay him back.

"O precocious child, I must be careful!" and he started for his promenade.

"Be sure to be back at one," was Ruth's reminder, and then the girls began to plan their "nice time." "I'll wash the breakfast dishes, Ruth, while you make the beds, you tuck the counterpane in so smoothly and have the pillows so straight," and Agnes, with sleeves pinned up and crash apron on, began her work. Her heart was very light, and as she worked she sang:—

> "Behold I come with joy to do
> The Master's blessed will;
> My Lord in outward works pursue,
> And serve his pleasure still.
> Thus faithful to my Lord's commands,
> I choose the better part,
> And serve with careful Martha's hands,
> But loving Mary's heart.
>
> Though careful, without care I am,
> Nor feel my happy toil,
> Preserved in peace by Jesus' name,
> Supported by his smile:
> Rejoicing thus my faith to show,
> His service my reward;
> While every work I do below,
> I do it to the Lord."

Ruth went up stairs and carefully spread the counterpane and arranged the pillows, but she did it mechanically. She was thinking of what Guy said about "fixing themselves up like other girls." She wondered if he was dissatisfied with their appearance, and if that could be the reason why he so seldom went out with them. Then he said they would become stupid if they did not go out more. If she could be sure he did not think them stupid now, she should not care. But he could not think so, for he had told her she was brilliant, and she knew she was gayer and more entertaining to him than to any one else, while as for Agnes, she was too good to be stupid.

"I should like to dress better just for his sake, now that he is a lawyer," she said with a little thrill of pleasure and pride. "Of course he will have a great many friends and they will have to see us sometimes. But—" here there was a pause and a deep sigh, "O, he does not know how little we have to dress with, if we would keep out of debt. There now, Agnes is singing and I am doing I scarcely know what," she added, as her sister's voice reached her. She did not hear the words, if she had heard they would have helped her. As it was, she chided herself for beginning the year so badly and hurried down stairs to help prepare dinner. Both she and Agnes decided it must be the very best dinner they ever had, for Guy liked good things, and on school days they had to live plainly. If the pudding was not *plum* pudding, it would be "almost as good," and they set to work gleefully stoning the raisins and beating the eggs.

"Wouldn't it be nice if we could live this way always?" said Ruth, as she put a large raisin in her mouth.

"Yes," replied Agnes, "but—"

"Now, Agnes, do leave the *buts* and ifs out once, and say that you would really like it."

"Well, yes, I am sure it would be very nice not to have to think and plan so much about our way of living, and sometime I almost wish we had more money for your sake and Guy's, but—I can't help it, it will come," as Ruth made an impatient gesture—"indeed, Ruth, I should almost fear to be rich."

"Why, for fear of losing your religion? I thought you had more faith."

"Yes, perhaps that is the reason, Ruth, my lack of faith on this point. If I consecrated all but my money to the Lord, I might fear, for it would not bring happiness with it, but God's grace can dim even the shining of gold to the Christian, so that neither the eye nor the heart may be held by it."

"It is when I look at the pitiful way in which it is doled out, even to Him who gave it, that I dishonor God by having such thoughts. After all, the grace of submission which we need, Ruth, is as hard to learn, as any lesson that might come with riches; don't you think so?"

Agnes left the room for a few minutes and Ruth did not reply. But the thought took possession of her mind. "The grace of submission, that is a hard thing to learn indeed, at least for some people. I wonder if any one ever submits *willingly,* or if it is not because when they reason about it they find they cannot do better. I don't know about this thing of having no will of your own: some people require greater strength than others. Now there are Agnes and I so very unlike; she could not manage and plan nearly so well as I. So it is necessary for me to have more strength of will because I have no one to depend upon. If we had more money it would be easier to be amiable and sweet, for then I should not be perplexed. But I must need a great deal of teaching, or rather a willingness to be taught, and that is the reason I can never see or feel like Agnes in spiritual things."

Such a sense of want, such a longing came into her soul, that she almost cried out; but Agnes returned, and driving back her emotion, Ruth went on with her preparations.

With the greatest care Agnes set the table, bringing out the best china, and arranging and re-arranging until she was sure everything was right, then she and Ruth found it was time to dress.

"Fixing up like other girls," still ran in Ruth's mind, and going to the wardrobe, she selected her maroon colored merino dress, because Guy said it suited her complexion.

"Your best dress and lace bow," exclaimed Agnes, who considered herself quite well dressed in her black alpaca, though it had been turned, and a blue neck-tie.

"Yes," replied Ruth, "my best dress and lace bow. Extravagant, isn't it? Promises well for the year?"

"One would think you expected somebody."

"So I do; a gentleman."

"O, Guy, you mean; but what is the reason you have your best dress on?"

"Indeed that is the very reason. I don't know for whom I should want to dress, if not for Guy."

"Of course, Ruth, we should do more for him than for anyone, but you are so careful of your good clothes, and so seldom wear them at home."

"Well, I have been thinking perhaps I had better pay more attention to my appearance. Fix up a little more to be like other people, I mean. One feels better satisfied with herself when she is looking well. And then, Agnes, as Guy goes more into society, I fancy he is becoming fastidious."

"Yes, I suppose so," returned Agnes, re-arranging her neck-tie. "How do I look, Ruth; does this dress look shabby?"

"Shabby! one would scarcely know that it is not new. You always look well dressed; but it takes a great deal of fixing to set me off."

Guy's face showed his approbation as he glanced over the table, and his "Why, girls, this is a feast fit for a king!" carried with it, greater pleasure, than the most graceful compliment from other lips could have done. After dinner they walked out together "to see the New Year," Guy said; and the girls felt sure that he must know all the great men of the town, he bowed to so many. Then he was not the least ashamed of his sisters either, Ruth thought, and she became quite animated, so that Agnes, who knew nothing of the reason, wondered at the unusually high spirits. *She* was very happy, for she was with the two she loved best on earth, and it seemed such a glad beginning to the year. She smiled, talked, and looked to where Guy pointed, seeing beauty in everything, even in the ragged children who begged pennies as they passed along, for an inward light gave the charm, and a sweeter voice than that of brother or sister, made gladness. Several visits were made that afternoon to old friends who urged them to stay for tea; and it would have been pleasant, the girls thought, but Guy appeared anxious to go home, so they yielded very cheerfully. Guy had been planning a delightful surprise for his sisters, and he meant to make the announcement at the tea-table.

"Now for home and an early tea," he said after making their last call.

The girls brightened at the thought that home was really becoming attractive to Guy, and although they had thought it would be pleasant to free themselves from home duties for one evening and enjoy it with their friends, they lost sight of their own wishes in their great desire to please Guy.

"It is the best place after all, isn't it?" said Agnes, looking at her brother, who was holding the door for his sisters to enter. But his hasty, "Yes, hurry up with tea, girls," gave a new turn to their thoughts. Perhaps after all he meant to spend the evening out.

"Wouldn't it have been delightful if we could have staid at Borden's?" asked Agnes, sitting down at the foot of the bed, her favorite seat, as she untied her bonnet.

"Indeed it would," was the reply. "I don't know when I ever wanted so much to stay. We might often go out for tea if it were not for Guy, and that is one reason I wish we could keep a servant."

"A servant would not be company for him, Ruth, he would not come home at all for tea if we were not here. But if he cared more for our friends he would be more willing to visit with us. I don't think, however men care to be from home at meal-time, and I am so glad Guy is not dissatisfied with our plain way of living, now that he sees so much style and moves in such a refined circle."

"Where would be the use in being dissatisfied, he knows it can't be helped," was Ruth's reply as she turned to leave the room.

"I thought you were hungry," remarked Ruth, as Guy refused one or two dishes that were handed him.

"Not very," was the reply.

"Well that was cool, hurrying us home as if you were on the point of starvation, and now acknowledging that you are not hungry," said Agnes, laughing.

"O, I only wanted you to have tea over soon, so that we could go out."

"Out!" exclaimed both, "where?"

"To the theatre, there is a splendid bill for to-night. Look your very best girls."

A deathlike silence followed this announcement, and as Guy had finished, he rose from the table and went into the parlor, leaving his sisters sitting there. When he had gone they looked at each other. "O, Ruth!" said Agnes, sorrowfully. And Ruth replied, sharply, "Well?" but it had a sound of pain as if she had encountered some terrible sorrow, yet meant to bear it.

"He will be so angry," continued Agnes. "O, I wish we had staid at Borden's. Hadn't we better tell him now that we cannot go?"

"You can tell him for yourself, Agnes," and Ruth began removing the dishes with as much haste as if she were eager to go.

"And you, Ruth?"

"I am going."

"Ruth, you certainly cannot mean it. Going to the theatre and you a Christian, and this is the first day of the year. O, Ruth, remember last night and your covenant." Her arms were round her sister now as though she would hold her back from evil, but Ruth shook her off, and ran hastily up stairs to the school-room. Locking the door, she walked up and down the room, with hands tightly clasped and a face expressive of the strongest conflict.

"Last night, and your covenant," yes, she remembered only too well. But was not she right in this? Guy *would* go to these places and he must not go alone. Her sister was the best one to go with him. He could never go wrong if she were with him. What was the use of praying that he might become a Christian, and leaving him to go alone as he chose. No, she would win him over. He should see that Christians did not have to attend church and pray all the time, for that would make him dislike religion, but that they were like other people, only better.

When all this was settled, she began her preparations tremblingly, thinking how very plain her dress would be compared with the handsome dresses, to be seen there, but determined to appear well for Guy's sake, and not to let him know the struggle she had passed through.

As she left the school-room and ascended the short flight of stairs leading to their bedroom, she heard Agnes and Guy talking.

"She is telling him," she said. "O, I wish I could be Agnes! but we are differently constituted, and there are different requirements made of us. Agnes does the praying, and I must make the efforts, the sacrifices."

Yes, Agnes was telling her brother. She had not to reason as to what was right or wrong in this case, having read that we are to shun every appearance of evil, and to keep ourselves unspotted from the world. Her heart beat fast, and her voice trembled, but not with indecision; for her soul was strong in its purpose to do right at all cost as she entered the room and said:

"Guy, I can't go to the theatre."

"What's the reason you can't?" was the surprised inquiry.

"Because our church does not allow it, and *I* do not think it is a good place."

"You don't! how do you know when you never were there? See here, Agnes, don't be a simpleton. Where is Ruth? I'll be bound she'll go; she has good sense and good taste. I saved up cigar money this week on purpose to take you. Hurry now, or we shall not get good seats."

"I can't do wrong, Guy; I must not go;" and Agnes went out of the room, back into the bright little kitchen where she had been so happy that morning. She wanted to go to her own room, but Ruth was there.

Guy was angry, very angry, Agnes thought, from his voice as he spoke to Ruth, but they passed out and she was alone.

CHAPTER III
GUY OR CHRIST

THERE are times when the soul isolates itself and is with God only; although in the midst of a multitude. Then, although seeming alone, it has companionship, it is not lonely. And there are hours of heart-felt loneliness, though surrounded by a crowd, when no look, word or touch of another can reach our hearts, so separated are we.

Agnes had felt all this, but never before did she feel such a complete and painful separation as when the door had closed and she was left. Ruth had made a sacrifice for Guy. She knew it must have been very hard to do it, and only her love for him could have induced her to go. But Ruth did not love him better than she. He would not understand that, and would think that want of love had prevented her from yielding. But O, if he could see her heart, if he could know how willingly she would give up her life for him, how gladly she would sacrifice everything but principle to satisfy him.

"And I can't tell him," she thought; "he would not understand it, but think I was trying to excuse myself, for we never talk like other brothers and sisters about our love for one another." Then came the question, "Why must I suffer and be misunderstood, when Ruth can act differently?" But again the voice was heard that ever brought calm and sweet assurance, saying, "Is this your love for me? He that loveth father or mother more than me, is not worthy of me, but he that loseth his life for my sake shall find it."

"O yes," was the response, "I would do a great deal for love of Guy, but more, far more for love of Jesus;" and so for His love she was willing to lose even Guy's love for a time if necessary, and could bear to be misunderstood if the Saviour trusted her. There was no shrinking from the thought of telling Him; no fear of being misunderstood there, so kneeling down, she poured forth the story. There were not many words, for as sometimes in opening our heart to a friend, we look up and catch a glance which tells us there is no need of further explanation, so she looked and felt that she was understood.

Earnestly she plead for her brother and sister. That *he* might soon learn to walk in other paths, and that *she* might lean more fully on Christ and less on her own understanding.

One thing perplexed her; that was whether she had better remain up until Guy and Ruth returned, and if she did, how she ought to act. It would not do to ask them about the performance, as that would revive unpleasant thoughts; and if she did not speak at all, they might think her in an ill humor. But she determined not to let this disturb her, the Lord, she knew, would help her to do right when the time came.

"Well, I declare! if she is not sitting up waiting for us," exclaimed Guy, quite gaily, with no sign of displeasure in tone or manner. "Weren't you dull? Confess now that you cried a little because you did not go? Look at her eyes, Ruth, didn't she?"

Not appearing to notice his last remark, Ruth playfully reminded her of her newly-formed resolution to rise at an earlier hour than heretofore, and told her to be sure and call *her* when breakfast was ready, for she was so sleepy she did not know when she should waken. Agnes good-naturedly promised to do so, provided she was awake herself, and ran up stairs, glad to escape from her brother. Ruth followed her in a few minutes, and going over to the dressing glass stood looking in. "How well you look to-night, Ruth," said Agnes admiringly. "I do not think I ever saw you with such a brilliant color. Did you enjoy yourself?" The question was put hesitatingly, as if she was not sure whether to put it or not.

"No, did you think I could? I can't even tell you what the play was, my brain was in such a whirl. But I laughed and talked and Guy was satisfied."

She sighed wearily as she laid aside her ornaments, and the tempter ever ready to take advantage, whispered to Agnes, "*She* suffers for her brother's sake, but *you* will not."

"No, not even for Guy, if it displeases the Lord. I must not let this move me," was the quick response.

There was no more said by the sisters that night. Agnes longed to help Ruth back to peace of mind, but Ruth did not seem disposed to enter into conversation, so there was only one way in which to do it, and her sister's case was given over to the One who alone can ease the burdened conscience, and Agnes slept undisturbed.

Ruth knelt as usual before retiring, but she could not reach up through faith to grasp the blessed promises; something kept her down and widened the distance between her and the Saviour. No sweet assurance came, for there had been other thoughts before those of pleasing Him. She had acted according to her own judgment and pursued the course she thought best.

She had not the comfort of knowing that He directed her paths, because she had not in all her ways acknowledged Him.

"I think it is the hardest thing I have to overcome, Ruth," said Agnes, as she came down quite late and found breakfast ready. She felt condemned and dissatisfied with herself, not knowing what to do, having prayed about it so often.

"How do you pray?" inquired Ruth, rather amused at her sister's distress.

"Why, I ask the Lord in faith to help me to get up."

"That is, you expect the Lord to set you right out on the floor?"

"O, Ruth, you are making fun."

"Indeed, I am in earnest; that seems to be what you expect. Now if I prayed about it, I should ask that I might have my senses about me when I was called, so that I might think what I ought to do, and *do* it. That is about as much as the Lord will do, and then if we fail, the fault is our own."

"Will you call me to-morrow whenever you waken, Ruth? I must have been making a mistake all along."

After that there was no more difficulty, and Ruth told her she was to be envied, having overcome her last failing.

"I wish I had," was the earnest reply, "but I have any number of faults that you do not see."

"Then I should not call them by such a hard name, if they were modest enough not to thrust themselves out to public gaze."

"You would not? It is only grace that keeps them within bounds, and I am quite as conscious of them as if they were seen. They do not, however, overcome me as they might if others saw them. But after all, Ruth, I think we often call things faults in others, that would be virtues, if we knew more of their lives and the motives that prompted their conduct."

"It is probable," said her sister, "but there is not much of this getting to understand each other's natures. There is not enough trouble taken to find one another out."

CHAPTER IV
LITTLE PHILIP

THERE never was a greater contrast than that presented by the two sisters in their mode of government. Entering the school-room of each, you could not detect the least difference in the order of the scholars, but while the result appeared the same, the methods were very different.

Ruth said "silence" or "looked silence," as the children expressed it, and there was silence. She spake and it was done, for the children well knew that she would have no disobedience. She was never unkind, and she loved children, though she seldom showed them her love; so if you had asked her scholars if they loved their teacher, they probably would have said they thought her nice and kind, for she did not whip, and she tied up their cut fingers.

It did not look dignified, some people thought, and they were sure Miss Agnes had no control over her scholars, as they saw her surrounded by them every day on her way to and from school. It was such an honor to carry her lunch basket, such delight to be first to meet her and have a place at her side. O, how they loved her! "She was the very nicest teacher that ever lived." And many even resolved not to study too hard for fear they should be promoted and have to leave her. Then when the time came for them to leave, such tears were shed at parting, that Agnes determined not to allow herself to be so loved in the future, and succeeded for a day or two; but it was strange, she did not know how it came, there was always the same ending.

Ruth assured her she would get over all that in time; but love was as necessary to Agnes as sunshine is to flowers, and among these little ones the pent up fountain found an outlet.

Ruth kept her love away, deep hidden from sight, when it became so intense that it was almost painful; in the other nature it kept bubbling up and running over whenever it found a heart that would receive it.

Agnes delighted in teaching, but Ruth, while just as faithful, taught because it was the best thing she could do, rather than from choice. But the duty was irksome, and often she longed to throw the book from her and give the scholars their dismissal. When such feelings possessed her, she "did penance," as she said, by giving special attention to the lessons, "for it would not do to have the children suffer from her whims."

One day there came to her school a little deformed boy, about eight years old. He had been brought there by one of the scholars, and when Ruth entered the school-room she did not notice him, but proceeded with the opening exercises. She had taught the children to repeat with her alternate verses of Scripture, and this morning selected the twenty-third Psalm. After she had repeated the first verse, the scholars took up the second. But there was one voice, clear and distinct, above all the others. Glancing round, she saw a pale face, whose large, earnest eyes, bent full upon her, touched her strangely. Slightly averting her head, she went on where the children left off, but still there was the fixed look. It was not a stare or look of curiosity, such as a new scholar might show, but penetrating as though the child had passed through deep experiences, maturing the intellect while the body was dwarfed and feeble. At the close of the exercises, a little girl taking him by the hand, led him up to the desk, and introduced him as a new scholar.

"What is his name?" inquired Ruth.

"I'll tell her; mother said I should be a man and speak out. My name is Philip Driscoe," and here the thin tiny hand was slipped in Ruth's. How very thin and white it was, like a baby's hand. As it lay for a moment in Ruth's the fingers closed over it, and stooping down she kissed the child. "I like you, you are good, like mother," and drawing closer he laid his other hand over hers by way of caress.

A sudden impulse seized her to take him in her arms, but the children were there, looking on understandingly. Holding both hands she bent smilingly down, but in an instant her eyes were full of tears. She was thinking of Guy. What if he had been thus afflicted? A thrill of gladness followed the pain occasioned by the thought, and collecting herself she took the child over to a seat in the middle of the room, promising him a book in a little while.

"And a slate and pencil to make pictures?"

"Yes, can you draw pictures?"

"O, elegant ones; mother says I'll make real ones when I am a man, if I don't die."

Ruth could not tell what to make of herself that day, or for many days after, she was so drawn toward that little face. "Now if it had been Agnes, it would have been quite natural."

But the truth was, wherever there was suffering or weakness of any kind, her heart threw off its casing, and she felt that she could do anything to shield or comfort. When the call came for strength or sympathy, she could give it unhesitatingly, but when there was only ordinary occasion, she made no response.

CHAPTER V
WHAT HAPPENED ONE DAY

AT the beginning of the year, Agnes had resolved not to let a day pass without having benefitted some one. "It may only be perhaps by looking pleasantly, or speaking tenderly, yet if done in the right spirit, the Lord will accept it and make it result in some good," she argued. And in the spirit of this mission she started for school one morning.

"What a wonderful thing it is to know that while there are millions of people on the earth, there is something for each one to do, that no one else can do. A work the Lord has laid out for each one of us," were her thoughts as she walked. But another thought followed: "How do you know your own work? you may be doing the wrong thing after all."

This was not the first time such a suggestion had been made. Once it troubled and bewildered her, but now her mind was clear on that point.

"For," she reasoned, "my work must be to do everything that comes in my way, as well as I can, without waiting for special calls. And if I do this faithfully, and the Lord sees that I can do a different work, he will turn my mind in the direction of it, and bring it near to me."

Her reflections were disturbed by the loud, eager voices of several of her scholars, who announced in one breath, "O, Miss Agnes, you ought to have seen Martha Nelson's father. He had his leg cut off, and they took him on a settee to the hospital, and Martha's mother is nearly crazy."

"How was it?" inquired Agnes, turning from one to another of the eager, frightened faces.

"Why, he drives a dray, you know, and he fell off when the horse was going fast, and the dray ran over him. Everybody says he was drunk."

"Hush, hush, we must never speak of another girl's father, as we would not like to have our own spoken of. Poor Martha, she will need to-day something that each of us can give her. What is it?"

"Pity," said one of the girls, who by look and voice showed that her heart was already touched.

"Is that all?"

"And love," was the reply.

"Yes, the dear Lord wants us all to do something for Him to-day, and as we cannot do great, hard things, He wants us to love and be sorry for Martha. And if we love people, we will do all the kind things we can for them; don't you think so, especially when they are in distress. And when we say our prayers, we must not forget to ask our Heavenly Father to love and care for Martha, now that her father is away from her, and may perhaps never get well."

When the lessons were over and school dismissed, Agnes hastened to the home of poor Martha. It was quite a distance from her own home, being at the other end of the town, and this was prayer-meeting night. But her day's work could not be complete until she had sympathized with these suffering hearts.

"Here it is, teacher," exclaimed the children who had offered to show her the way, "The house with the shutters shut tight."

Knocking, and then trying the door which she found unfastened, she entered the darkened room, having told the children it would not be best for them to go in on that day. A sad disappointment, for they had meant to kiss Martha and tell her they were sorry, and hear all about the accident, although some of them had witnessed it.

Passing into the back room, Agnes found Mrs. Nelson and her children surrounded by a half dozen neighbors, in the midst of a discussion as to the position of the poor man when he fell. The one who had the floor at that moment was a tall, vigorous looking woman, who evidently had battled hard to occupy her present position. She had gone as far as: "'Says I to my man, there goes Bill Nelson;' and says he to me, 'Yes, there's no fear of his old woman letting him over-sleep himself; she's too smart for that'; when, all at once I seen him fall with his head to the horses' hind feet and——" here the entrance of Agnes, whose knock had not been heard, caused the speaker to subside, and a general movement of chairs and stools to take place.

"O, it's teacher, mother," said Martha, springing to meet her, light coming into her heavy, swollen eyes.

"And how do you do, ma'am; it's kind of you to come. And it's a sorry day this has been."

By this time chairs had been backed until they could go no farther, aprons smoothed, and the sleeves of the tall orator pulled down. Then there was silence, Agnes having taken one of the three chairs offered her.

"Yes, Mrs. Nelson, this is a sad occurrence. You have need of a great deal of sympathy, and I am sure you will have it." As Agnes looked round the room, and saw the various expressions of countenance at this remark, they appeared so ludicrous that under any other circumstances it would have been hard to control herself. As if encouraged by her notice, the tongues were again set in motion, and to her horror she was having all the details of the accident.

Martha had drawn her stool beside her teacher, who now took the opportunity of whispering comfort, and telling her how much her school-mates loved her and sympathized with her.

"I knew you would come when school was out, but it seemed so long. Did anybody have to be kept in?"

"No, the scholars were all quiet and attentive to-day; they were thinking of their little school-mate."

At these words, meant to comfort and reassure, the child laid her head on her lap and broke into loud sobs. Agnes thought she had done harm rather than good, and the tears sprang to her own eyes. Placing her arm round the child, she drew the bowed head up and let it rest on her.

"Poor thing," whispered the neighbors, "she takes it hard."

With a great effort Martha looked up into her teacher's face and said: "I wasn't thinking about father then."

Not knowing but what the child might have some trouble that she could relieve, Agnes whispered: "What were you thinking of? Don't fear to tell me; perhaps I can help you."

"O, teacher," and there came a great sigh, "you help me all the time. Nobody ever was like you, and it was because you were so kind I had to cry."

There were other wet cheeks than Martha's then, and Agnes was already repaid for her long walk. With a few more kind words addressed to Mrs. Nelson, she rose to go, and Mrs. Nelson followed her into the other room.

"How can you manage without your husband? Had you anything but his wages?" she inquired, feeling that sympathy at this time might perhaps require a stronger expression than words.

"That is just what I've been thinking of, Miss, if I could get time to think. They are well meaning, you see," pointing toward the other room, "but they have no considerateness. It's not for me to sit down and be grieving over what can't be mended, but to be looking round for a way to bring bread into the house. For as you asked me, Miss, I'll just tell you. We haven't even had all his earnings; if we had, this wouldn't have happened to him. But I'll not hear a word said against him there," with another glance toward the back room. "I'll try, if God spares me, to keep starvation out, and maybe when he is lying there, something good may come into his mind."

"If you could only spare Martha to live out at service for a while, she might help you. At any rate you would have one less to feed," Agnes ventured to remark.

"That is just what came into my head this afternoon, Miss. The one next to Martha is old enough to take care of the rest when I am out, and if you could hear of a nice place where they wouldn't be too hard on her, I'd be a thousand times obliged to you, if you'd speak a word for her. She sets great store by you, and a word from you as her teacher, would do more good than if I'd talk for a week."

Agnes promised to do what she could, and then timidly, but earnestly, reminded her of the sure help in the time of trouble, the one whose friendship and love are equal to all our demands. By the time she reached home, Ruth was becoming anxious, for when Agnes intended going anywhere after school, she always announced it before leaving in the morning.

Knowing that her sister would probably be uneasy, and that she should have little time to prepare for church, she almost ran home; so that when she entered breathless, her face a deep crimson, Ruth's tone of alarm, as she exclaimed, "What is the matter, Agnes!" brought Guy immediately into the room.

"O, nothing Ruth; please wait until I breathe;" and she tried to get up a laugh. "I did not know I was so out of breath. If you wait a minute, I will explain," for Ruth was beginning to protest that something was wrong.

"There now," she said, removing her hat, and leaning back in the rocking chair, "I am ready to put your fears to rest." Then followed an account of the accident and her visit to the family.

"See here, Agnes, it is all very well to sympathize with people in distress, when you don't have to sacrifice yourself; but you are not called upon to do more than you are able to perform. And it is quite enough for you to teach school, without running to see all the youngsters whose fathers get tipsy and break their legs," was the opinion Guy gave after hearing her story.

"What do you charge for advice, Mr. Lawyer?" she asked, laughingly, as springing up she advanced to the table and begged Ruth to hurry with the tea, for she was "as hungry as a hawk."

Guy followed, declaring that "if all clients were as self-willed and independent as she, the lawyers might pull down their shingles, take a last look at Coke and Blackstone and then— —"

"Well, and then?"—queried Ruth, very much amused.

"Why— —then go to grass."

"Little boys should not use slang," said Agnes, demurely.

"Neither should little girls act contrary to the wishes of their big brother," was the reply.

After a blessing had been silently asked, Agnes said:

"Do you really think I am self-willed, Guy?"

"Of course I do; it does not require a knowledge of law to decide that."

"How do I show it? I never meant to be so."

"Well, you succeed pretty well if you don't. I should not like to see you make the effort, if that is the case. How do you show it? Why, by thinking you know better than other people. Don't she, Ruth, and acting out her thoughts?"

"You are partly right and partly wrong," was the reply. "Agnes is not in the least self-willed. It is I who may be called that. In this you are wrong. You are right in saying she acts out her thoughts; but you give a wrong reason. It is not because she thinks she knows better than others. She does not trust her own judgment nearly as much as either you or I."

"Now don't you begin to be mysterious, Ruth, if she don't, whose does she trust?"

"The Lord's."

"Oh!" and Guy had no more to say. Agnes could have embraced her sister then. She wanted to say something to Guy about Ruth, because she knew her better than even he or any one could know her. But he was so silent now, perhaps this was not the best time. Guy ate a little, Agnes thought, and she did not feel so hungry after all; so when Ruth had finished she said:

"Let me wash the tea things myself to night, Ruth, I have not been doing anything all day. I will be ready in time for church." She plead as eagerly as if asking a great favor, and Ruth amused at her childishness, with a warning about not placing the glasses in too hot water, ran up stairs, little thinking of the effect her words had either upon the one for whom they were spoken, or the one to whom they were addressed.

"If we had Martha Nelson, she could do so much for Ruth when I am at school," thought Agnes. "But the money, where is that to come from?" Turning it over and over in her mind, she could see no possibility of having Martha, but somehow there was an impression that Martha should be with them. On the way to church, she decided to speak to Ruth about it.

"Did you ever have impressions that certain things *should* be, Ruth, and yet the things seemed impossible?"

"I scarcely understand you," Ruth replied. "What kind of things? spiritual?"

"No, spiritual impressions of temporal things, I suppose. But this is why I ask." Then she told of Martha's mother wanting to find a place for her, and of the impression amounting almost to a conviction that she was to come to them. "Only I can't see where the money is to come from."

"How much does her mother want a week?" asked Ruth, thoughtfully; for when Agnes had these impressions, they generally had weight with her sister. Indeed she sometimes felt as if the Lord told their Agnes more than almost any other Christian; that she was peculiarly favored of God.

"I did not think of asking her, but it can't be much, for she is young and will require to be taught. Why do you ask, Ruth?"

"I hardly know; perhaps if she did not want much, we could take her."

"Well, I shall ask her mother without giving the reason, and then if it is best, the way will be made clear."

CHAPTER VI
DEATH,—THEN LIFE

MRS. Nelson will be willing to let Martha go to a good home for her board and clothing until she learns enough to be entitled to wages, Ruth," Agnes joyfully announced. After a little consultation as to whether their old dresses could be cut down for her, and some misgiving on the part of Ruth as to the training of such a mere child, when neither of them could devote much time to her, they concluded to make the trial.

"If she's worth anything she will be worth a great deal to me just now, for it will enable me to do what I have long been planning, without seeing any way to accomplish it," thought Ruth.

Martha, poor child, in her great joy at the thought of living with "Miss Agnes," seemed to have forgotten the painful circumstance which compelled her to leave home. But on the day that her mother finished patching her few clothes, tying them up and telling her she might go at once to her new home, there came sad tidings from the hospital. They need never hope to have the husband and father home again, unless to take one last look before they buried him out of sight.

"Let me stay with you, mother; Miss Agnes will not be angry, and you will be so lonely," plead the child, forgetting everything else in the one great thought of her mother's approaching widowhood.

"Yes, I will be lonely," wailed the mother. "God only knows the loneliness and heart-ache that is in store for me. But we'll not shed tears now, child, there'll be time enough by and by. We must away to to see him; he'll have a word to say to us I'm thinking."

She meant to be brave, and to keep back the tears until "by and by," but the thought of hearing the last words, perhaps, or what was worse, finding him unable to speak to her, completely unnerved her, and the strength she had all along tried to keep for her children's sake, failed her. In the midst of this scene, while Martha stood beside her mother, wringing her hands and beseeching her not to groan so, Agnes stepped in, having had but one session of school.

"What is it?" she enquired, alarmed. "Your father is not dead, Martha?"

"I don't know, they sent word that he was dying, and we are going to him. Won't you go, Miss Agnes? I am afraid," and the child shuddered as she spoke.

A shudder passed through Agnes, but she said: "Yes, I will go with you, but I must find some of the scholars to send home and tell Miss Ruth." She thought with horror of going there to the hospital, where men and women were lying struggling for life, to be followed by their wild, staring eyes, and their cries of entreaty for relief. For a moment she was possessed with the feeling that she could not encounter the fearful sight, and the question arose: "Why need I cause myself to suffer when I cannot relieve the sufferings I shall witness?" But ashamed of her cowardice, she banished the thought as unworthy a place in her heart, glad to be able to share the sorrows and help to comfort those whose time of trial and sore distress had come.

"I shall need help one day, perhaps," she said to herself, "if Ruth or Guy should be taken first. But I pray God that I may die before them, unless—" here the child-like-spirit showed itself, and her soul became suddenly strong—"it would be to His glory that I should thus suffer."

A boy was sent with a message to Ruth, and then, as Mrs. Nelson was ready, they set out on their mournful visit. It was a long and silent walk. The heart of the sorrow-stricken woman was too full for words, and Agnes, so young and unaccustomed to such scenes, did not know what was best to say.

The hand that held Martha's tightened its grasp as they came within sight of the hospital, and although the voice was very low that whispered in the woman's ear, "Be strong, God will help you," it gave courage and re-assurance.

Up the broad steps and through the long corridors they passed; Martha trembling and drawing closer, while Agnes dared not look to the right or left. Presently they stopped before a curtained recess, and drawing aside the curtain Mrs. Nelson passed in. Martha wanted her teacher with her, she said; but when she was told her father might have things to say to his wife and child alone, she withdrew her hand and followed her mother. It was not long, however, until the nurse came out with a request for Martha's teacher.

"He wants some singing, Miss, and the little girl told him you could sing beautiful," said the man. As Agnes stepped near the bedside, Martha called out eagerly, "Here she is, father, this is Miss Agnes."

He tried to speak, but it was only a movement of the lips, no sound came. Sitting where he could see her, Agnes began in a low, clear voice, to sing:

> "There is a fountain fill'd with blood, —"

When she came to the lines—

> "And there may I, though vile as he,
> Wash all my sins away, —"

the dying man held out his hand as if beckoning her over. Again his lips moved, and stooping she heard: "Again—sing."

As her voice arose again, slowly repeating the words, her heart made supplication for the soul so rapidly passing away. Hymn after hymn was sung, all speaking of Jesus and his great love for sinners, and to Agnes it seemed that Jesus was himself speaking in each. She knew he was there in the midst of them, and wondered if the sick man saw him. Bending down, she whispered: "O, how the Saviour loves you; do you love Him?"

He looked at her with the strange, earnest look the dying only have; the look that seems to be measuring eternity; and then his hands were raised and clasped, while his eyes remained fixed on hers.

"He is asking you to pray," said the nurse; "He is near gone."

There was no time to listen to Satan now, or to think of anything but this soul venturing out into the unknown future. Was it prepared?

O, how she plead for him! As if face to face, she talked with God. The Holy Spirit gave her words and great assurance; it seemed as if the answer must come. He had promised to hear and to give the things desired. He had *never* refused to listen to the feeblest petition, and here was a burdened soul; was not the Saviour near, to take from it its burdens? So she entreated as though she alone could save him, yet knowing well that Jesus alone had power to forgive sins.

They had been sobbing around her, but she did not know it. Now there was a strange silence, a sudden calm, and she felt that she had prevailed. As they rose from their knees, something about the dying man attracted them. While they had been kneeling, Jesus had drawn near and whispered to him. The power and music of that voice were ringing in his ear; the beauty of His smile was flooding his soul and radiating his face. In that moment he had passed from death into life.

His wife and child looked at him with awe; the nurse drew back as if the place were too "holy ground" for him. Only Agnes and the new-born soul understood it. But it had only caught a glimpse of the Saviour; before long, with the same indescribable expression, it passed away to be "forever with the Lord."

They went home silently as they had gone there; but a new feeling had taken possession of them. They had seen strange things; new thoughts had been given them, and death had not to them its old terror, for they had seen it swallowed up in victory.

CHAPTER VII
GUY GIVES HIS VIEWS IN FULL

MARTHA was fairly installed as kitchen-maid, to the great delight of Agnes, while Ruth congratulated herself that there would be no more dishwashing for her, a thing she detested above all others. "She appears anxious to learn, doesn't she?" asked Agnes. "She was a good scholar and perfectly obedient. I think you will like her, Ruth. If we gain her affections I am sure she will do anything for us."

"But then we must be careful, Agnes, it does not answer to pay too much attention to servants. They are sure to become consequential and to value themselves too highly, if you notice them much."

"But she is a child, and everything is strange. Besides, when she thinks of her father and of separation from her mother, she must be sad, and perhaps may try your patience. I shall help all I can, but she had better look upon you as mistress. Be patient for my sake, sister."

There was no reply to this, and Agnes was afraid she had made a mistake in proposing such a child, instead of one more fully grown. That night after Martha had gone to bed, she slipped up stairs to know if she had repeated her prayers.

"O, yes, ma'am, I always say them; I should be afraid to go to sleep if I did not."

"We have a great deal to thank God for, Martha. Every day He cares for us, and it is the least we can do to thank Him. Do you thank Him for what you have, or only ask to have more?"

"I guess I ask most for the things I want. I forget about thanking, only I mean it."

"Yes, and God sees that you mean it, but He expects you to tell Him so. Now if I were to give you a great many things every day, and you did not thank me but were all the time thinking of other things you desired to have, I should call you ungrateful and not give you any more. Don't you see how it is? Now when you are praying, be sure to ask not to be allowed to forget pleasing God, by doing every thing as if He were here looking at you. Are you warm enough child?"

"O yes, ma'am, Miss Ruth came up and tucked me in nicely, and—"

"And what?"

"She kissed me and said 'good night.'"

Agnes's first impulse was to exclaim with surprise; but checking herself she stooped down, saying: "And I must follow Miss Ruth's example, I suppose. Be a good girl, Martha, and Miss Ruth and I will be your friends."

"I need have no fears; Ruth could never be anything but kind, although people so often misunderstand her and think her stern. She will never let generosity carry away her sense of justice; and after all that is the better way," thought Agnes, as she descended to the sitting room. Guy was home that night. As Agnes entered the room he laid down his book with the remark: "I say, Agnes, brother Snowden is considered the salt of the earth among you church people, isn't he?"

"I suppose he is a good man; I don't know much about him. Why do you ask?" was the reply.

"Well, only that it strikes me *that* kind of salt would not make very strong pickle."

"How you talk," said Ruth, "You know nothing about his Christian life."

"O, that is it, he has two lives has he? Well, I admit that I know nothing about his *Christian* life. But I do know about his business life, if that is a separate and distinct thing. When a Christian comes to me and asks me to undertake a case that is simply trickery and fraud, then I want to know how he can separate himself from his profession of religion. I thought religion had to run through one's life, instead of hinging and unhinging it when one chose. I know one thing, that some of your church members dabble in puddles so dirty that I would not touch them with the tip of my finger, and this Snowden is one of them."

"I would not judge the many by one," replied Agnes, quietly.

"No, that is a wholesale way of speaking," said her sister, positively. "And you may not have understood the man, Guy; and you know you are rather hasty."

"See here, Ruth, don't you begin to take sides with that fellow. Agnes is bound to defend him, because he is a goat of the same fold. But you may be glad you slipped out, backslid is the word I believe, for it is no honor to have the association of such a contemptible specimen of mankind."

Ruth's face flushed and her eye kindled at his allusion to her backsliding, but she did not speak, while Agnes, who was deeply pained at his unkind speech, immediately replied: "You are wrong, Guy, Ruth is a church member, the same as I. And while neither of us can endorse what is done by every member of the church, we know there are good, earnest Christians there, and it is not for us to sit in judgment upon any."

"Bravo!" he exclaimed. "This is most animating. It is a pity you were not a man, you would make a capital advocate. But excuse me, I forget, we have ladies in the profession. If you have no objection to reading with me, I shall be proud to present to the bar such an able pleader."

This was just what Agnes wanted, to have the conversation turned. So that Ruth and the church escaped, she did not care what was said of her. For fear of Guy returning to the old subject, she inquired whether he thought women could ever attain any eminence in the profession.

"Yes, the fact of them being women will not mentally disqualify them," he replied. "As a general thing they are clear sighted, and although not always logical, have a way of carrying their point in spite of all opposition. To office work some might be well adapted, but when it comes to practise at the bar, to get up and harangue a crowded court-room; to be brought in contact with low characters and take any part in criminal proceedings, then I say a woman is out of place. When they take that stand I shall step aside and let them glory in their shame."

Guy spoke with great warmth. Ruth appeared to be listening attentively, though she did not speak. Encouraged by the interest manifested by his sisters, Guy Gorton Esq., Attorney at Law, was in the act of giving a fuller expression of his views, and by his *logical* reasoning, determining woman's position for all time, when the door-bell rang and Martha ushered in visitors.

To Ruth it was a happy relief, for though she had appeared to manifest interest, very painful thoughts were passing through her mind. She had made a great sacrifice for Guy in hope of doing him good, how great, no one knew, and yet withall she had failed in her object. He looked at her as the world always judges of Christians; not by profession but practise. However, it may sneer and cavil at doctrine, the world is not slow to recognize and respect the character that like pure gold carries with it not only beauty but sterling worth.

"Bartered my Christian character," she thought, "and what have I in exchange? Complete failure, dead loss;" and all through the evening, though she talked and laughed, the question and answer came up before her.

When their friends had gone and the girls went up to their room, each sat down on her favorite seat as if for a talk. With Agnes it was the foot of the bed, having the low post on which to lean, while Ruth took the low rocking-chair. The thoughts of both ran in the same direction, but neither seemed inclined to break the silence. Agnes would have spoken, but Ruth was sensitive, and any allusion to the subject might pain her. Suddenly she said, "What a lovely character Edith Hart was, Ruth. Her manners are charming, and she is perfectly sincere, I am sure. Did you notice what difference Guy paid to her opinions and how much he seemed to admire her? I wish he would fall in love with her and marry her, for of course he will marry some one, and she would have such a good influence over him."

"Yes, when they were married she might, if he in the meantime had not exerted a wrong influence over her. It must require a great deal of grace to maintain your Christian integrity, when those you love are worldly minded. I don't think Edith would hold out any better than the rest of us, if she loved Guy as she should. But there is no use in talking about that, it will be a long time before Guy can marry."

"Why, his practise is improving, isn't it? I often hear him talk of his clients, and you know lawyers charge very high for advice. I don't know where I heard it, but I am of the impression that they will not give the least bit of advice under five dollars. At that rate, you know, he will make out well."

Ruth wanted to laugh at her sister's simplicity. Do as she would, she never could teach Agnes the value of money. And now, poor child, she seemed to think Guy had nothing to do but open his mouth and gold dollars would roll out, as diamonds did in the wonderful story of "Toads and Diamonds." In one way she was glad that Agnes knew so little about money matters; she wanted to save her from care or anxiety. But there were times when she was so perplexed and straitened, that it made her impatient to think any grown person could be so stupid as to live in their house and not more fully understand their circumstances. At such times she murmured and even rebelled, wondering why she should have all the burden. It did not reconcile her to it, to know that others admired and deferred to her judgment. She grew tired of thinking and planning, and longed for a strength greater than her own, upon which she could lean, for some one to help her bear the burdens. This was not sentiment. If the thought of marriage came to her as it probably did, especially at such times, she put it far from her. She would never leave Guy and Agnes; but if they only had been constituted differently, they could have helped her. And they in turn, little dreaming of her struggles, looked at her with admiring eyes, giving her credit, as far as they could follow her, and thinking what a wonderful woman their Ruth was.

"But it is slow work after all," she said, by way of reply to her sister's remarks. "A man must possess great talent and still greater patience and perseverance, to arrive at any distinction; and until he reaches that, he cannot expect to make his fortune. There are so many young lawyers, they are crowding each other out."

"But Guy must be satisfied, Ruth; he does not appear troubled or disappointed."

"Why should he? he is like hundreds more, and that fact is consoling. Besides, the slower and more cautious he is in the ascent, the more assured will he be when he reaches the summit."

She rose as she said this, and Agnes thinking the talk was over, removed her arms from the friendly bed-post. But she had only gone over to the bureau for her Bible, that she might read a chapter as usual before retiring. Returning to her seat she abruptly asked: "Do you think much about the future, Agnes?"

"Do you mean about heaven?"

"No, the future of time."

"Not nearly as much as I used to. Before my heart was renewed, I kept looking to the future for something satisfying; but it never came until I found the Saviour."

"Yes, but I mean do you wonder what your life is to be, and what changes will come to us all?"

"O, often such thoughts come, but they are disquieting, and I drive them away. It is better to live by the moment, just as we breathe."

Ruth opened her book and began to read. Her eye having fallen on the last verse of the sixth chapter of Matthew, it had called forth the above question. Now she read it all carefully; it was just what she needed to-night. Dissatisfied with herself, and feeling that she was not satisfying others, she wanted to find the rest that comes from leaving everything in a Father's hands, but she was yet to find the spirit of trust and submission.

CHAPTER VIII
THE YOUNG PEOPLE'S ASSOCIATION

RIPLEY, like most towns of its size, possessed few novelties, and rarely produced a sensation. It did its duty in the way of gossip, as towns and villages are expected to do. Carrying out, in a manner peculiar to some, the injunction of the apostle: "Look not every man on his own things, but every man also on the things of others." When the Rev. John Jay was called to the Fourth street church, the whole town partook of the excitement, for he was a young and single man; moreover, he came from a distant city, with the strongest recommendation. He had been there about a year, when the community were again aroused to a high pitch of expectancy, by the following announcement one Sabbath morning: "The Official Board of this church will hold a special meeting at the close of the Wednesday night prayer meeting. A full attendance is requested as a matter of grave moment is to be presented."

As the minister made this announcement, he fervently wished they would always attend to business after prayer-meeting. He would not then have to refer so often to that means of grace, for the Fourth street brethren looked well to the temporal interests of their church.

He did not see the nod given by brother Smith to brother Snowden, which said:—"I told you it was a comin'; now you'll believe me;" nor the succession of nods in return, which indicated:—"Well, to think of it. After that I give up." Neither did he overtake the group of officials who slowly wended their way homeward in earnest discussion, shaking their heads, and trying to give greater force to their words by an energetic movement of the hand and arm.

He was picking his steps as best he could through a crowd of children, who were darting here and there, looking up at him with beaming eyes, and trying to touch his hands at least, if they could not hold them. As he looked at these lambs, he wondered if there could be love for the Saviour in any heart which did not make the young a special care. After he had parted from them, two little feet came tripping back to remind him of his promise that he would finish the story of Moses in the afternoon. He went home thanking God for the innocence of childhood, while with their noon-day meal many of of these children partook of poison administered by their parents. For what else is fault-finding, intolerance and uncharitableness, but the deadliest poison?

And what gave rise to this, was simply that the young people of the church and community wanted to organize a Young People's Association, at the suggestion of their pastor, and wished the privilege of holding it in the Lecture-room. The thing was projected so suddenly, that very few of the older members knew anything about it until it was brought to their notice in this manner.

When the hour for the evening service arrived, there were few who had not heard the news; for brother Smith and brother Snowden considered it a good Sabbath day's work to discuss the matter in all its bearings with all the members they could meet, although they did not doubt but the women folks would be sure to side with the young people.

On Wednesday night the Lecture-room was crowded. Those whose faces were seldom seen in the Lord's house, and many of the brethren who always found it extremely inconvenient to attend on that night, were there. Of course, none but the Board could remain, for the meeting, but the others could hover round and catch the news much sooner than if they had staid at home.

The Rev. John Jay drew very near to Christ in presenting his flock, and most earnestly prayed for the young of the congregation and community, many of whom he saw there for the first time. As he prayed, brother Smith and Snowden were loud in their responses.

Those who went to meet the master of assemblies, felt it good to be there. Unto them had been broken the bread of life. Unto them a well-known voice had spoken, and now they were stronger, braver and more hopeful. When the minister, with uplifted hands, pronounced the words of the benediction, like the gentle dew, fell that peace into their hearts, drawing them out in tenderest sympathy toward all His creatures.

After it had been ascertained that there were no intruders, and the doors had been carefully closed, the business commenced. Prayer was dispensed with, for there had been so much of it before.

"I move we dispense with everything but the business in hand," said one, and as the meeting concurred, the petition was presented by one of the most promising young men of the church, named Hayes. In it the petitioners set forth that they, feeling the need of proper social entertainment and mental improvement, wished to organize for that purpose, and most respectfully asked the use of the Lecture-room.

The secretary had no sooner uttered the last sentence, than brother Smith arose and protested against any such desecration of the Lord's temple.

"Social entertainment! What did that mean, but a parcel of boys and girls without a speck of grace in their hearts, wantin' a good courtin'-place where their father's and mother's wouldn't see them. For his part, no child of his should join them.

"There's carryin's on enough under our very noses, in the hearin' of the word without givin' any more license," he continued, waxing warmer.

"That's so," said brother Snowden, and one or two others grunted an assent.

Then the young man named Hayes arose and calmly said: "It is well known that the young seek enjoyment. Their minds are fresh and active; they will turn in one direction or another. We cannot control them; we can only seek to guide them. Many of our young are going to ruin, because there are no well directed efforts put forth to meet the wants of their impulsive natures. The world offers to gratify them. It stretches out its arms and says: 'Come to me. I have pleasures for all at my command.' And already many have turned and accepted the proffered good. We Christians groan over these and talk of their final doom; yet what do we offer those, whose eager, hungry natures cry out to us for bread?

"We say, 'Go to church on the Sabbath, and to prayer-meeting; that is well; but they want more than this and so do we. That will do for the spiritual part of our nature. But there is a social and intellectual part which must be cared for. And let me tell you, brethren, until the church makes provision for every want of the young, it can never gain a proper hold upon them.

"It is not for me to stand here as the teacher of those older and wiser than I. But it seems to me if we had the Apostle Paul here, he would define our duty in broader and more decided terms. And still a greater than Paul says: 'What man is there of you, whom if his son ask bread will he give him a stone?' That question applies to every want of the being. How are you going to answer it to-night? I charge you not to close your doors upon those who knock, lest, if the gate of heaven closes upon them, you be found not guiltless."

These pointed words evidently made a good impression, and the opposition had not courage to oppose farther. Several of the brethren, men whose hearts were under divine control, and whose lives were devoted to the advancement of the Master's cause, in a few words endorsed the remarks, and when the question was called for, there was but one side, the opposition not voting.

When the young people were called together, there was quite a large gathering. Rev. John Jay was unanimously elected President, and Mr. Hayes, Secretary. But now the great difficulty was, to obtain members. All at once, these young men and women, the latter especially, became conscious of their ignorance, and dreaded its exposure, for the public Library of Ripley, was not very extensive or attractive. Its old volumes of Theology, its Annals and Histories, had been too heavy matter for youthful digestion, and as a majority of the young women did not consider it necessary to know anything of the affairs of the nation, or to possess any knowledge of the world outside of their own town, they had been content to glean from the newspapers, to note the deaths and marriages, watch for some new recipe in cookery, or the love-stories as they appeared each week.

After a great deal of difficulty, twenty signatures were obtained, with the understanding that the young ladies in preparing their essays, were not expected to read them or make public their names. Every thing at first, until the members acquired more confidence, was to be voluntary. After the business of the evening had been transacted, a call was made for contributions.

This was at once responded to by the principal clerk in the principal grocery store, he giving them in loud and thundering tones: "The Star Spangled Banner." So grandly did he render it, especially the "bombs bursting in air," that one young lady covered her face to shut out the view of the descending bombs, and the President was compelled to move aside, to prevent, if not the deadly missiles, the bodily weight of the speaker from descending upon him.

Loud applause greeted him at its conclusion, and but for the hint given by the President that it was time to close, they would have been favored with another brilliant display. The general opinion expressed by those having any knowledge of theatricals was, that it was "almost as good as a play," and the orator of the evening was overwhelmed with compliments. After this, there was little difficulty in obtaining members; indeed the young clerk the very next day succeeded in getting fifteen, so that by the following meeting night, there was a large and expectant assemblage. The young grocer held forth of course, and several others were so stirred with patriotism that Fourth of July orations and patriotic speeches followed each other in close succession. With a great deal of persuasion, a few ladies were prevailed upon to sing, and thinking the music should correspond with the addresses, they were about to give Hail Columbia, when the President suggested that something else by way of variety would be acceptable to the audience.

"The Old Arm Chair" was substituted and gave general satisfaction. Even old brother Sneddinly, who with a few others was at a side door listening, declared that anything that brought the Bible into it, must have been written by a Christian; and if it wasn't in the Hymn Book, it went pretty near as slow and solemn as some of the hymns. The latter assertion could not be contradicted by his companions, and they even went so far as to congratulate the pastor on his success in getting up "so big an affair." "Suppose you add still further to its success by your presence and assistance," he suggested with a smile; "we need some wise and clear heads among us."

But that thought could not be entertained for a moment by the brethren. "How would it look for them to be mixing in with a parcel of young folks, most of whom made no show whatever of religion? O no, that would be too great a compromise! There ought to be a strict line drawn between the world and Christians."

"Isn't there danger of drawing it so tight that we will cut them off from us entirely?" asked the pastor.

"No fear of that," was the reply, "if it is held tight at one end, the other end will be loose enough to slip them through."

"Thank God," said the Rev. John Jay, mentally; "there shall be no tightening or straining at this end!"

The Association soon became the all-absorbing topic of the place. The young people discussed it, and the old people discussed it. It was destined to become a grand success, the Rev. John Jay thought, as he saw denominational prejudices give way and the young people of the different churches unite to help one another and be helped. Yet there was one drawback; some of those for whom he was most anxious, whose feet had begun to travel the downward road; the children of those who professed to be God's children, were never seen there. His soul was troubled. He knew at whose door the fault lay, yet what could he do? He was young and inexperienced. These men and women, parents of the prodigal ones were older than he. Should he show them the fearful mistake they were making in condemning everything that was not purely a religious worship? Should he tell them by reason of their sternness and their narrow prejudices, which seemed more to them than the souls of their children, they were driving their children away from them and from God? Would they bear this from him, even though as Christ's ambassador he were to speak? He was exceedingly doubtful; perhaps they might dismiss him. Wouldn't it be better for him to remain and watch over these wayward ones, showing them that he knew the weakness of human nature and the unquenchable ardor of youth? He concluded to try it. He would make that his one great work; he would win them to Christ. With a heart somewhat lightened, he gave himself out more fully in loving words to the young, and entered more earnestly into every plan suggested to make the association an attraction. But just as he was seeing the good results here, in another direction the storm was gathering. He saw it in the black looks and averted eyes of many of the officials and even of their wives, but as yet its mutterings had not reached his ear.

Some to whom he had endeared himself heard, and were fiercely indignant that such a sweet, Christ-like spirit, as their pastor's, should suffer pain through such allusions.

Just the very thing he had labored to accomplish, was that which was to testify against him. Many young hearts had been drawn nearer to Christ through him, and their voices were heard in the songs of praise which went up from that little prayer-circle on Wednesday night. But these pious men and women, although rarely ever present themselves, saw nothing in which to rejoice. On the contrary, they mourned over the weakness of one, who by virtue of his sacred office, should be far removed from such things. Wasn't it too evident that the young women went to church to see the young pastor, and the young men to see the young women? It was time such things were stopped; they were a shame and disgrace to a church.

In the meantime the society was flourishing, a new element had been brought into it, and so far as its literary character was concerned, the most sanguine expectations of the Rev. John Jay had been met.

Several public meetings had been held, filling the house to overflowing, and eliciting the highest and most deserving praise. But that was of course from outsiders, and those simple-minded souls in the church, who never see evil without looking for good; who indeed are always finding the latter in everything and in every one but themselves. These were not competent judges. "Had the church been left to them, where would have been its sacredness and sanctity? Why, they never even changed their voices in the Lord's house, and they even wore a smile while there, as if they had forgotten the Lord was in his holy temple."

Thank God, there are those who carry His image about wherever they go! Such need not by their own effort show a conscienceness of His presence. He is the continual light of their countenance, and the gladness and music he makes in their hearts, is heard in their voice. They worship and praise with every breath, because their souls must find an outlet to the great love which holds them.

CHAPTER IX
A DAY OF PLEASURE

IT was an unusually warm day in June, and Ruth had dismissed her scholars early on that account. She stood by the window plucking the dried leaves off the climbing rose, and thinking how delightful the approaching vacation would be, when a little hand touched her. Looking down she found Philip by her side.

"And what will mamma say at having no little boy at home?" she asked, drawing him nearer, and smoothing back his wavy hair.

"O, mamma knows. She only said I must not trouble you. I guess I wouldn't do that, though, because I love you too much."

Here the little hand tried to give Ruth's a great squeeze, while such an effort brought color to the pale cheeks. Not only that, but it brought something he wanted very much, a kiss.

"You always kiss me for telling you that, Miss Ruth, and so does mamma. What do you do it for? Do you like little boys to love you?"

"You have not told me how much you love me," was the laughing reply. "I cannot answer questions till I know all about them."

"O, I love you more than all the world, except my mamma;—isn't that *ever* so much?"

"Yes, that is a great deal. Then you don't love any one but your mamma and me?"

"I love God," and the earnest eyes were fixed on the blue clouds. "Would you like to be up there, Miss Ruth? Mamma reads about it for me. I should like to go up there and see it. I should like to see God, too, but I would come back again, you know. Mamma always cries and hugs me when I say that; just as if I would stay away from mamma and you. I guess I wouldn't. But I would see all the beautiful things the Bible says are there, and then I would draw pretty pictures. Mamma says there is a house up there for us all, and some day we will go and stay there. Do you want to go, Miss Ruth?"

"Yes, some day," she replied; but there was no kindling of the eye, no joy of soul at the thought, for Ruth knew that her earthly love was stronger and more absorbing than the heavenly. "There, now, we will go and see about Miss Agnes's dinner," she added, glad to divert his thoughts.

"Miss Agnes has not come, Martha?" she inquired.

"No, ma'am. I have been watching for her. She will be awful hot, I think."

"You are Miss Agnes's little girl, and I am Miss Ruth's little boy, aren't we?" asked the child.

"I am Miss Ruth's, too," said Martha, decidedly.

"Yes, but you love Miss Agnes best."

"I love both just the same—only different; but Miss Agnes was my teacher."

Ruth gave such a quick look, that the child drew back frightened, thinking she was angry; but she smiled at her, and Martha's fear left her. How much a smile will do, and what a very little word or act will bring that smile. So when Agnes came home "awful hot," as Martha said, she was met by smiling faces, and waited on by loving hands, and finally it ended in a "real party," for they all had strawberries and cream, to keep Miss Agnes company.

"Isn't he a darling," whispered Agnes, glancing toward Philip, who was intent on his strawberries.

"Yes, he is a remarkable child; his mother must be very fond of him. I have been planning something to-day, Agnes, for all hands," looking round at the children, as she spoke.

"What?" asked her sister, brightening.

"I can't tell you until we are alone. But it will bring the roses to somebody's cheeks, and be very nice for all the somebodies."

"Don't let us do any thing this afternoon, but talk or read," proposed Agnes; and hearing this, Philip hurried to the school-room for his own little chair, so that he might lay his head on Ruth's lap and listen. But *Christus Consolator* was too profound, and lulled by the sound of Agnes's sweet voice, and Ruth's caressing touch, he slept.

"When the sun goes down it is time for little birds to be in their nests," said Ruth, and Philip now wide awake and knowing what was to follow, ran to tell Martha to get her hat. The first time he had staid, Ruth sent word to his mother that she would take him home, and ever since it had been understood.

"One on one side, and one on the other," he said, as he placed himself between Ruth and Agnes, offering a hand to each. But Ruth asked what was to become of poor Martha, and soon the two children were talking as gravely, and looking as demurely side by side, as if they had been grandfather and grandmother.

On their way home, while Martha walked before, Ruth developed her idea, which was that they should have a pic-nic, perhaps several of them during vacation, "as it would be so expensive to go away for a length of time you know. Just a family affair," she continued, "and we will take the children along to enliven us."

Agnes fell in with the plan very readily, and pictures of ferns, mosses and lichens at once rose before her delighted vision.

There were trying days still to be passed in the school-room, days on which Ruth felt it would be a relief to scream out or do something desperate. But when she looked at the little ones under her care, trying to be good and obedient while under control, she chided herself for her impatience, at the same time relaxing her discipline. But the days went by and the holidays came, and Miss Ruth's joy at her freedom was not one bit less than her pupils'; though she didn't run screaming to tell every one that "school was broken up." "We might as well go soon, Ruth. I feel as if I could scarcely breathe here," said Agnes, a few days after school had closed.

"A day won't help you much if you are in that state. What shall you do all the other warm days?"

"Imagine I am in the woods," was the laughing reply.

"Then you had better bring your imagination to bear upon it now. Guy will have to dine down town that day. I fancy he will not like it very well, for he is so fastidious. Guy was certainly meant to be rich."

"Why not ask him to go with us?" suggested Agnes.

"If you want to be laughed at you will. Imagine our Guy going with two women, two children, and a lot of baskets, to spend a day in the woods!"

"I should think he might enjoy the change quite as much as we. But men are queer, they look upon women's pleasures as childish, I really believe."

The day before the pic-nic every one was busy; even Philip insisted upon helping. When Guy came to dinner there was such an air of commotion that he at once inquired the cause.

"What's up, girls? house-cleaning? If that's the case, I'm off; no soap-suds and white-wash for me."

"Hear him; house-cleaning in July!" exclaimed Agnes.

"I do believe, Guy, you men would never do a bit of cleaning all your lives, if you were house keepers."

"You may bet on that," was the reply. "That is just where we would show our good sense."

"Your filthy habits, you mean."

"Well, either, whichever suits you. But you haven't said what was in the wind."

"None came this way to-day, we could not tell."

"We are going to close the house to-morrow, Guy, so you need not come home to dinner. We intend going to the woods to find fresh air."

But Guy didn't like the idea; it sounded common, he thought. Every day he met a lot of women and their babies, with a parcel of brats following them, going over the river or somewhere. "Why can't you take a week each of you, and go to the country like other people?"

That, "like other people," was too much for Ruth, and she said, sharply: "We can't be what we are not. Beggars must not be choosers."

Guy replied in as sharp a tone that "some people liked to make a parade of their poverty," and finished his dinner in silence. This unfortunate affair threw a damper over the girls, but the children did not come within the shadow of the cloud. Ruth had a sudden angry impulse not to go at all, scarcely knowing why, as it would not spite her brother. But she could not yield to such a thought when the happiness of Agnes and the children was to be considered.

Agnes spoke very little after the occurrence, knowing what state of mind Ruth was in, but she sang in a low voice some of her sister's favorite hymns, and in a little while the cloud rolled away, the sun came out, and the storm was all over. By tea-time Guy and Ruth were as if nothing unpleasant had happened, but there was no allusion made to the pic-nic.

"I wonder how people feel who are going on an extended tour," said Agnes, as they filled their lunch baskets.

"That depends very much upon the people themselves," replied Ruth. "This little trip is giving us more real pleasure than some people would know in travelling all over the globe."

"Yes, I suppose so; it is the appreciation that is needed, and without that there can be no enjoyments."

Fortunately, for Guy, he did not see the party set out the next morning, or the shock might so completely have overcome him as to unfit him for any business whatever. But they waited until he had gone, and then they started with their baskets, trowel, and garden-fork.

"People will take us for herb-gatherers, and think these are our children," said Agnes, gaily.

"Shocking!" exclaimed Ruth, with mock earnestness.

They took the boat for several miles down the river, to the great delight of the children, especially Philip, whose keen eyes took in the smallest white speck of a sail, and then when they had climbed a very little hill, and gone down a big one, they were in the woods.

"What a delightful perfume! Isn't it charming!" exclaimed Agnes, delightedly, as she sat down by a tree to "enjoy herself." But the children who had been scampering about, declared there was a much nicer place not far off, and so Miss Agnes, who could imagine no scene more charming, very reluctantly consented to tear herself away.

The spot chosen by the children was indeed lovely. Perfectly level ground covered with the richest moss, out of which rose broad flat rocks, and along side of which, not many yards distant, ran a clear little stream on whose banks the feathery fern grew, and into which it dipped its graceful frond. On the other side of the stream the wood was more dense, but through it a broad path led to a bend in the river.

"We need go no farther," exclaimed both Ruth and Agnes. "Nothing could exceed this for loveliness and shade.

"By the river of Babylon there we sat down," and Agnes once more settled herself.

"There we hung our harps upon the willows," added Ruth, throwing her shawl on a branch overhead. "Now, Agnes, let us take it easy and make the most of the day, for such days will be like angel's visits."

"Well, suppose we rest first. Methinks I could forget myself in sleep."

Presently Ruth was accosted with, "I think I know now what I should do if I were rich."

"What?" she asked.

"Take sick people into the country. That is, if I could afford to keep a carriage. I have been thinking about it since yesterday."

Ruth knew what had brought it to her mind. Guy's picture of the women and their babies; sick, of course.

"Yes," she said. "Many of those who die every year might become strong and well again, if they could be taken from the close, stifling air of their wretched homes into that which is pure and fresh."

"Nothing could give greater pleasure than to have these poor, emaciated babies and wan-faced women look up at you with a smile, as if saying, 'O how this cheers us.' I wonder if it will ever be?"

"'Tis hard to tell," was the reply. "But suppose you had a carriage, your husband might object to your using it in this way."

"Then I should not use it at all." Here Agnes looked as if at that time rejecting its use.

Ruth laughed. "Wait, my dear, until you get it," she said. "Or before you give yourself away, it would be well to ask the gentleman, if, in case you owned such a thing, you could use it for such purposes."

"Not I indeed. No man ever finds me asking him such a question; what was *his* would be mine. But I shall know, when I see the man, what *manner* of spirit he is of."

This occasioned another laugh, in which Agnes joined, and the two, banishing the thoughts of sick babies and pale-faced women, had a gay time. In the meantime, the children had scrambled over rocks to gather lichen, and dug holes deep enough to bury a kitten in, in their efforts to get moss; they had sailed little nut-shell boats down the stream, and in the many ways that children have enjoyed themselves. Everybody was hungry of course, so by the time Agnes was ready for her ferns, there were empty baskets in which to place them. But they read and talked before that, and walked through the woods on the other side out to the river, finding several beautiful plants on their way. Then at the last the ferns were gathered, and Agnes did wish they could have had more baskets. But Ruth informed her she might have gone home by herself if she had.

"Now that is my idea of enjoying oneself," said Agnes, as tired but very happy, she laid her head on her pillow.

"Yes, that is rational, sensible enjoyment," replied Ruth. "I wish sensible people would have the moral courage to act sensibly in this matter of rest and recreation. But it would shock a great many quite as much as it did Guy. Now I think it is well and often necessary for persons to have a more decided change, when their health requires it, and their means will allow. But this thing of going to fashionable resorts, for the sake of appearance, spending hundreds of dollars in mere dissipation; coming home envious and dissatisfied at the greater show made by others, instead of seeking change for the good of it, at the same time having their hearts drawn out after those less fortunate, is to me one of the greatest evils of the day."

CHAPTER X
MISS SMITHERS COMES, AND A SURPRISE

WE had better engage Ann Smithers," said Ruth, after several old dresses had been cut down and made over for Martha. "She knows so well how to manage, and has patterns of the styles. With our help she can accomplish a great deal in a few days."

"Do you think we can get new dresses this Fall? We have worn these faithfully, you know?" inquired Agnes, as she examined and re-examined her suites.

"Not for some time, I fear; it takes a great deal to keep up a house these times. But it does not seem fair that you should give your money to me, Agnes. In future you had better keep what remains after paying for your board. It is not right to have you work hard and get so few clothes."

"Do you get any more, and haven't I as good a right to do without things as you?"

"No, it is different. I keep the house, and perhaps things are not managed well. I don't know. I get bewildered at times to know which is the best way. But now that we have Martha and she understands her work so well, I intend to give music lessons this Fall. That will be a great help."

"And yet, when you think *you* ought to do this, you want *me* to keep money from the house, so that I may have new dresses when I choose. O, Ruth, could you think me so selfish!"

"It would not be selfish, it would be right," urged her sister. But she could not bear to tell Agnes that if it were not for Guy they might both dress differently. He had come to her repeatedly for money to help him out of difficulty, and now he said there was no manner of use in attempting to do business up three flights of stairs; he must have a ground floor, and of course that would involve greater expense.

"If you could only manage to start me in this, Ruth," he had said, "there is no reason why I should not succeed. These one-horse affairs are always failures. I will pay you back again when money comes in you may be sure, as there is no doubt it will."

Then Ruth, who could not resist such pleading, told him to make the change and she would help him out with his rent, resolving then and there to do extra work in order to meet the demands upon her. She reasoned in this way, that if she chose to make sacrifices for Guy, Agnes need not share them, and if she told her she surely would insist upon it. And that was the reason she thought it best for Agnes to keep part of her own money.

"How little she suspects," she thought as Agnes sat down to rip her dresses, looking quite satisfied at having to do with her old clothes. "What a sweet spirit our Agnes has."

Agnes worked and thought. She did not have the least idea how the money went, but she knew a little more would not be amiss, so she said: "If there was any other way in which I could help you, Ruth."

"Never mind that," was the reply, "you can direct Martha, and see to things when I am out, that will be a great help; for although Martha does remarkably well for a child of her age, there are many things to be attended to, requiring a more mature judgment."

"Quarter day" came, and when Agnes handed Ruth her money, it was returned except the sum kept out for her board. "You know it was decided that in future you should have your own money, Agnes."

"But, Ruth, I don't understand. Why should I when yours all goes for the house?"

"If it were not best, I should not urge it," was the reply, and Ruth seemed so positive that Agnes yielded. Weeks rolled on and to every inquiry made by Agnes as to the time when Ruth meant to buy herself a dress for winter, there was some trifling excuse made. Finally she told Agnes there was no necessity for her waiting, it would be better if she bought hers now before school commenced, and she could get her own whenever she was ready.

"What kind would you get if you were in my place?" asked Agnes, a new light breaking in upon her.

"A poplin by all means, they will be worn altogether."

"That is the very thing," thought Agnes. "I am sure now that she does not mean to get any dress this winter, and she is so fond of good clothes. Our Ruth is the most self-sacrificing woman, I ever knew. Now it would be different if it were I, for I do not care for dress in the same way as she; but I am so glad I thought of it, she shall have one after all."

Full of this thought she set out to make her purchases. After looking over several pieces, she came to one that was just what she wanted for Ruth, a rich brown of beautiful quality. But the price perplexed her, she could not get two and pay so much for them.

"Have you any others of this shade?" she asked.

"They are much coarser," was the reply, as the salesman handed down several pieces of inferior quality. After a great deal of thinking and calculating, Agnes ordered a dress of the fine material and one of the coarser. "Will you oblige me by laying the fine dress pattern aside for a few days until I send for it?" she asked. "I will pay for both now however." Then giving Miss Smithers' address for the other, she left the store and was soon at Miss Smithers' door.

Everything was explained. How that Ruth never would think of herself, and it was time some one should think for her, and then Agnes arranged the time for having them made.

"When mine is cut so that it cannot possibly do for Ruth, I shall have hers sent. I can hardly wait for the day," she said, with the delight of a child. "Please cut my skirt before then, Miss Smithers, for Ruth will think it coarse and insist upon my sending it back, unless it is cut. But it will make up quite prettily, and in winter no one notices the quality of your dress." Guy would have been amused at her business capacity then, had he heard her.

Such a time as she had when she went home. Ruth could not understand why the dress was sent to Miss Smithers', instead of there. "Just as like as not you have been cheated," she remarked, "and then when the skirt is cut there is no help for it. To be sure it will be an assistance to have some of the cutting done."

Then came Miss Smithers and the dress. With assumed calmness Agnes showed it to her sister, but not without many secret misgivings.

"There, isn't it pretty, Ruth?"

"Yes, very, but it is extremely coarse, Agnes. Why didn't you get a *good* dress? You have enough second-best ones for this winter."

"This will answer nicely now, I like it. Besides, I did not want to spend all my money on a dress."

"Well, if you like it, and as long as it is cut, there is no use in making you dislike it. It is all well enough if it were not such a poor quality."

Late in the afternoon, when there was little more to be done by the sisters, the rest being Miss Smithers' special work, Agnes asked Ruth if she could spare Martha to go on an errand for her. Handing her a note and telling her to take it to the address and wait for an answer, Agnes sat down to await the *denouement*.

"O dear, I wish it was over," she thought. "I am almost afraid to show it to her. I feel as badly as if I had done something wrong. Is it ever right to deceive? Of course this does not harm any one, and I did not see any other way in which I could manage it; but after all it was taking advantage of Ruth, and it may give her pain instead of the pleasure I intended." These and many other questions passed through her mind as she sat waiting for Martha. Presently she appeared with the parcel.

"Open it, Ruth, it is yours," said Agnes, determined now to face it at once. "I bought it and mine at the same time, but I kept it purposely until to-day."

Ruth was so touched by this thoughtfulness on her sister's part, that she was a long time in untying the cord. She did not want to look up just then, for her eyes were full of tears.

"Let me," said Agnes, and she drew it away from Ruth. "It is almost the same shade as mine," she said, holding it up to Miss Smithers.

"Well, now, so it is," replied that lady, laying down her work and taking the new dress pattern. "They are as nearly alike as two peas. If people did not know you so well, they would take you for twins."

"O, Agnes, it is ever so much finer," exclaimed Ruth. "What did you do that for?" She spoke as if it pained her, and Agnes laughingly replied: "Because, big sisters should always have the best things. Now don't look so doleful, Ruth, one would think you were going to be beheaded. I declare, Miss Smithers and I would be bowing and smiling like Frenchmen or Frenchwomen, rather if we were having a dress presented to us."

Ruth laughed and bowed, and then Miss Smithers made one of her characteristic speeches and so, "it was over," at last as far as Agnes was concerned.

Not so with Ruth. She could scarcely command herself for the rest of the day, she was so deeply moved by this thoughtful act of her sister. "And to think of her wearing a common dress just for the sake of getting me a handsome one," she said.

"Dear Agnes, if she only knew what thoughts I have had about having to do without things sometimes, she could never love me enough to make this sacrifice. I suppose it was providential; God had a hand in it. But that is the strange part, that He should reward me after all my complaining."

These were soul-expanding thoughts, and had Ruth but taken them to God, praying that they might be made the means of drawing her into a closer union with Him, what a wonderful change would have passed over her. As it was, they gave such a softness to her tone, and such gentleness to her manner, that Martha, quite encouraged, ventured to express her admiration of the dress, of the giver, and of the receiver, in such a mixed up way, that Ruth was forced to laugh outright.

"I got a beautiful idea the other day, Agnes," said Ruth, as she sat stitching her dress. "One who had been speaking of her Christian life, said, 'in looking back she saw some triumphs achieved, some enemies slain.' While a friend replied that, 'in place of every foe that had fallen some grace sprang up.' I had not looked at it so before; it is a beautiful thought."

"And comforting as well as beautiful," said Miss Smithers, with moistened eyes. "But Agnes, here, don't know so much about this thing of fighting as we, Ruth."

"If I don't, then I am not living a Christian life," replied Agnes, earnestly. "For the Bible says we must war a good warfare, and if I am not doing it then I must be in sympathy with Satan. Miss Smithers, Christians make great mistakes about each other, often. Because we do not see each other's struggles, we think there can be none. Now when I have the most to contend with, I do not talk most about it, for no one can help me but God."

"Yes, to be sure that is true. But it is a most wonderful relief to me to speak. When I have anything on my mind it has to come out. But you are so gentle and placid like. I really thought you were not like other people."

"Well, now you will know, in future, that I am like other people in my struggles, faults, and—"

"Bless me, not faults. I never saw a fault in you, all the time I have known you."

"There is a great deal in living with one to know them. Ruth can tell you that."

"Everything," said Ruth, emphatically as she left the room.

In matters of dress, the girls seldom approached their brother. Perhaps because they so seldom had anything new. Then he liked showy dress, and theirs was always moderate. But at night, after Miss Smithers had gone, Ruth could not help exhibiting her poplin, and telling what Agnes had done.

"Now that is what I call pretty," he said, when Ruth threw it over her shoulder. But when she told him it was a gift from Agnes, a deep crimson overspread his face. In a few minutes it was gone, and looking at Agnes steadily, he said in a peculiar tone, "How much you women are capable of doing."

Neither of them understood him, but there was something in his face and voice that deterred them from questioning him, and Agnes replied with a smile, "I am glad you like it, Guy. I treated myself to one at the same time, and it is made up ready to wear."

CHAPTER XI
THE YOUNG PEOPLE'S EXCURSION

RUTH and Agnes had joined the Young People's Association, and now there was to be a grand excursion. Such an excursion as had never been seen in Ripley. Guy had become acquainted with the Rev. John Jay, through his sisters, and as that gentleman had united his entreaties with theirs that Guy should accompany them, he was at last prevailed upon. It happened to be the very hottest day of the season, although the latter part of August, and although Guy had several times declared to himself that he would "back out" of the affair, the extreme heat decided him. "He would go with a pack of monkeys to the moon, or anywhere, for a breath of pure air." Of all the gay parties that ever set out from Ripley this was the gayest. Scarcely a breath of air stirred. People were astir because their business compelled them to make some exertion, but they moved about listlessly, as if the mere act of living were a labor rather than a pleasure.

The excursion was to start from the church, where already there was quite an array of omnibusses drawn up as much in the shade as possible. So when six young people came up breathless, their faces flushed and eyes sparkling, hoping they were not too late to get a seat, they did *so* want to get among the green fields, out of that stifling place, the horses pricked up their ears, and the sleepy drivers brightened up, having come in contact with the freshness and charm of those glad gay natures.

"We can't make very good time to-day, no how," said the driver of the coach they were about entering. "It's going to be as hot as blazes."

"All right, driver; we're in no particular hurry. Any time this week will do," said one of the young men as he clambered in.

"Isn't it delightful, none but ourselves," was the exclamation. But just then Guy, Agnes and Ruth appeared, and took their seats. By this time the other coaches had been filled, the word was given, and the party started off amidst cheers and waving of handkerchiefs. It was for the time as if a fresh breeze had suddenly sprung up, giving new life to the town through which they passed.

"Can't you turn into a by-road soon," said one; and "O, please do, it is excruciating going over these cobble-stones," said others. But the heat had not quite dried up the driver's fun, or else the street was in very bad condition, for just as this was said, they were bounced up like so many rubber balls, and the driver, with a twinkle in his eye, remarked that there could not be more than a mile or so of that kind of road.

"Are there any undertakers along this road?" asked Guy, seriously.

"Undertakers! what do you mean, Guy?" said Agnes, quite shocked at his levity. The whole party set up a laugh in which the driver heartily joined, knowing what had called forth the remark.

"I merely thought we would require the services of one, if not more, at the rate we are going, especially as there is a mile more of such road."

In the midst of another laugh which followed this speech, the coach turned off into a shady lane where the trees on either side almost met, forming a delightful shelter from the sun, which was now pouring down its rays most lavishly.

Through sun and shade the horses kept up their trot, the driver being called to repeatedly to be kind to them, until the joyful announcement, "The woods, the grand old woods!" was made. Just at the entrance to the woods stood a hotel. And the arrival of the coaches made quite a stir at the "Cross Keys," as it was called. The proprietor was aroused from his slumbers under the old chestnut tree at the end of the house, where he had been vainly endeavoring to fix in his mind some of the previous week's news; judging from the paper which lay on the grass, and the spectacles which, just resting on the tip of his nose, seemed ready to follow the news,—by the barking of the dogs and the scampering of servants.

"Bless me," he gasped, "if there ain't a load. Pretty plucky whoever they are to travel this sort of weather." And gathering up himself and his glasses, he made as great speed towards the front of the house as his roly-poly figure and the heat would admit.

By the time he reached it, black Pete, whose business was to attend to the stables and do a little of anything needed about the house, stood cap in hand, grinning and bowing to the party who were alighting.

"Nice kind of a day this, friend," said one of the young men, as Pete took his station near the horses heads. "No heat to speak of up this way, I suppose."

"Just a little, sah!" and Pete's grin was broader than ever, while he rolled his eyes in the direction of the girls. "It feels a good sight breezin' since you come sah, de young ladies, I mean." Here there was another bow, and the whole thing, the bow and the compliment was so overwhelming, that the girls ran laughing up the steps, almost upsetting the worthy landlord.

Presently they were followed by the young men who had staid behind to have another word with Pete, and then those who had not brought dinner, among whom of course were Guy and his sisters, made arrangements with the landlord for that meal, urging him to bring out everything his larder contained, in view of the fact that a party of ravenous wolves were to be fed.

"This weather don't appear to set very hard on you at that rate," he replied, his fat sides shaking with merriment as he went off to obey orders.

Then Guy and a few others began to search for a cool place, in which to eat dinner. First they tried the house, but it was so dark they could not see, and when the shutters were opened the flies swarmed in; next they tried the porch, but the glare was too great. Some were beginning to be cross and unamiable, when Pete's head again appeared.

"If de ladies and gen'lemen wants a nice cool place, there's one over yonder in de arbor."

"O, yes, come and take tea in the arbor," sang the girls, as they bounded down the steps and followed Pete, whose delight appeared to equal theirs, for although the sun could not penetrate the closely interwoven vines, which covered it, neither could the air, had there been a breath stirring. But it was "romantic" all thought, and Pete agreed with them; though I question whether if he had gone to the stake for it, he could have told what the word meant. There was one thing he *did* know, however, and that was, that if they remained out of doors, he could enjoy their society, and it was not every day such a rare treat was his. So while the party sought the woods until the time for dinner, Pete went to bring out "de table and cheers," thinking of the good time he was to have, "listenin' to de grand talk of dem town folks."

At the appointed hour the "wolves" sought their prey.

"I guess dat here will do to begin with," remarked Pete, drolly, as he deposited on the table two large dishes of chicken, and a plate of tongue.

"Yes, that will do for the first bite," was the reply, of one of the young men. Pete showed his ivories and darted off again. But on the return trip he had an assistant, and between the two the board was amply spread.

"I'll just be rusticatin' round here, Susan, so you needn't stay," he said, as Susan announced her readiness to "fetch them anything else that was needed."

The girl looked at Pete, then at the party. Her look of inquiry was met with: "O, no, there is no need of you waiting, if we require anything he can get it."

Pete made a bow, and Susan, glad to be relieved, thanked them and retired. Pete would have acted in full the part of waiter; already he had installed himself behind the prettiest young girl's chair, but he was requested to seat himself outside and keep his ears open in case of being needed.

Seating himself on the top step of the summer-house, and leaning his back against the lattice-work, he obeyed orders by listening intently to all the conversation. He evidently favored the ladies, from the nods of approval and looks of delight which he gave at their remarks.

It certainly could not have been from the conversation that he was reminded of angels; perhaps the bright, fair faces of the girls and their light attire suggested it, but he began, during a little lull in the talking, to hum:—

> "O, gib me de wings of de angels,
> To fly away, to fly away,—"

before he had gone farther, there was an exclamation of delight; "Don't stop, sing it all, it is splendid!"

Pete chuckled and after wriggling round to where he could see without being seen, and clearing his throat several times, took up the strain again; this time in a louder key, and with the swaying of the whole body, where before it had only been the movement of the head.

> "O, gib me de wings of de angels,
> To fly away, to fly away,
> O, gib me de wings of de angels,
> To fly to my heabenly home.
> Thar thar ain't any sorrow nor sighin',
> Thar thar ain't any sickness nor dyin',
> But de Lord will himself wipe de tears from our eyes,
> When we fly to our heabenly home.
>
> O, gib me de wings of de angels,
> To fly away, to fly away;

O, gib me de wings of de angels
To fly to my heabenly home;
Thar we'll all be dressed up in white raiment,
And keep walkin' along de gold pavement,
And we'll each hab a crown and a harp in our hand,
When we fly to our heabenly home.

O, gib me de wings of de angels,
To fly away, to fly away;
O, gib me de wings of de angels,
To fly to my heabenly home.
Thar we'll sing hallelujah foreber,
And keep wavin' our palms all together,
And the Saviour will say, 'Come sit down by my side,'
When we fly to our heabenly home."

By the time Pete had finished he was in a state of rapture, swaying from side to side as though in fancy he were mounting upwards on angel's wings. But he was brought out of his ecstasy by the shouts of

"Bravo! well done for you, Pete."

"Where did you learn it?" eagerly inquired Agnes.

"At de camp, Miss," was the reply.

"Why, were you in the army, or were you a slave?" another asked.

Pete rolled his eyes until nothing but the whites could be seen, as he said, "At de Camp-Meetin', you know. No, ladies, I never was a slave only to old Satan. Dat was enough of slavery for dis here darkey."

"Say, now, tell us how he treated you, that's a good fellow," said Guy, handing him some loose change out of his pocket. "This is for singing, now go on."

Poor Pete's face grew very grave. "It ain't very pleasin' to tell of, and ef it's jest de same, I won't scare de ladies with talkin' about it."

"But we wish it," they said, and as there was no help for him, Pete began.

CHAPTER XII
PETE'S SLAVERY AND FREEDOM

WELL, it's rather flusticatin' to tell grand folks like you about a darkey what's of no account, but I thinks of it considerable when there ain't much else to do. You see I had a father and a mother, and my father wasn't of much account for he drinked like a fish. Then he walloped us all round, and come pretty near killin' the whole of us like he did mother."

"Killed your mother, the wretch! what did you let him do it for?" asked one of the girls excitedly.

"Couldn't help it Miss; but I'm comin' to that. Well, you see he got drunk and walloped us, and mother said she weren't going to slave herself for a animal like him, so when he came home drunk she wouldn't give him nothing to eat, and that made him furiouser.

"Mother said he might bang till he got tired, so she used to lock herself in her room and take us with her, and then when he got tired cussin' and swearin' he lay down and went to sleep. Mother worked hard enough, I tell you, to get bread for us all: you see there was six of us, and it took a powerful sight of wittles. She never said nothin' about workin', though, only when father broke up the cheers and things, and then she used to cry, and we all cried." Here Pete drew his hand across his eyes, and the girls looked pityingly at him. In spite of the pain caused by such recollections, they were so curious to know all, that Pete was again urged to go on.

"Well, I helped de best way I could, for I was a little shaver then, and Jim, he was next to me, he did little jobs for de white folks around. But father he got worse, and wouldn't work no how, and he was always gettin' took up, and then when they let him out of jail he was furiouser than ever. One night, O laws! I most wish I'd never gone and been born when I think of that, mother and all us children was asleep. Father had been took up, and so we wasn't afeard of nothin'. It was a snowin' and a blowin' sky high, and nobody could hear nothin' for the wind. All at once I felt somethin' a movin' over my face, soft like, and then it made for my throat. Then I ups and gives a spring, and run into mother's room, but somethin' tripped me, and I fell down right on top of it. Then it moaned out like, and—and I knowed it was mother a lying there, and that somebody had killed her.

"I began to call 'murder' as hard as I could, but father, it was him did it, got a hold of me again, and told me he'd soon shut up my fly trap. I know'd he was goin' to do it, so I give an awful leap and sprung clear over his head and right out in de snow. I know'd he wouldn't go far to katch me, for he'd have enough to do to clear hisself, so I waded along till I come to de man's house that Jim worked for.

"He had two awful fierce dogs, and one of them made a spring at my throat while de other caught hold of my leg and took a bite out. De man, hearin' de dogs, put his head out of de window and asked what was de matter. So, as I couldn't speak, I just groaned, and he told de dogs to lay down. Well, he came down and took me in de house, and all I could say was 'Father,' and 'Murder.' So he called up de rest of de men folks and took them over, but when they got there father was gone, and mother and de baby was dead. Poor mother, she was holding de baby tight to her bosom. De other childerns was screechin' and cryin', and de door was wide open, and they was nearly frozen. Well, de poor house buried mother and de baby, and took all de children but Jim and me, and de man Jim worked for said he could stay thar as long as he wanted help. I hadn't no place to go to, so I worked where I could, and that wasn't much because it weren't de time of year for work, and I slept in sheds and barns, wherever de folks would let me.

"Mother she was a good woman, and made us say our prayers every night, but I didn't say 'em any more after that night, because I didn't see de use of prayin' to God when he let my mother get killed. I hated God then and I said so to Jim, only nobody else talked to me about them things, and I didn't get a chance to tell 'em. It was a good many years that I went on that way, only I got steady work. One summer de fellows said thar was goin' to be a camp meetin' somewhar near, so I concluded to go and see what it looked like. So I sets out on Sunday mornin', and when I seen de white tents, and heard de people singin' and shoutin', I thought it was de curiousest thing I ever seen. I got along tolerable well, talkin' to de colored folks what waited on de tables, when all at once a big horn was blowed, and everybody went off to preachin'.

"I went too, jest to look on, and when de preacher give out his text he said, 'Thou God seest me.' I didn't think I need to be afeard, for I didn't steal nor nothin', so I looked him square in de face. But by and by I began to feel queer, and then I begin to look down on de ground. It appeared as ef old Satan was a tryin' to drag me down to de bottomless pit, and I know'd ef he'd git me thar once, he'd take care to hold on to me pretty tight. I was afeard to look down, expecting every minute to be swallowed up, and I couldn't look up for I know'd God was looking at me. All at once something appeared to pull me down, and thar I lay while de people was a singin' and a prayin' all around. After a good spell somethin' spoke and says: 'Look up, Pete;' and I says, 'What's wantin'?' Nobody didn't give no answer, so I begin to groan agin. Then somethin' spoke agin louder, and says: 'Don't be afeard, Pete, it's me.' I kind of looked up, but didn't see nobody lookin' at me, so I felt worse. Then the third time somethin' says: 'Rise, Pete, your sins is all forgiven.' I says, right out loud; 'Who says so?' and de same voice, only sweeter and more lovin' says, 'De blessed Jesus; you needn't to be afeard any more.'

"I tell you I jumped up quick, and began to laugh as hard as I could. Some of de people said I was crazy, but de pious folks said I had got a blessin'; and so I had, de blessedest blessin' ever I got. Dat's about all, ladies and gentlemen," and Pete, bowing, betook himself to clearing the table.

The Rev. John Jay, who with the rest, had been an attentive listener, now said: "To be able to tell that last part, my friend, is worth more than all the world to a man; 'for what will it profit a man if he gain all the world and lose his own soul, or what will a man give in exchange for his soul.'"

"That's so, sah," replied Pete with glistening eye, "he wouldn't be of much account no how."

Several more hours delightfully spent in the woods, and then the coaches were announced, and the homeward road taken, but not without a parting word to Pete.

"Good-by," called out the girls as they drove off, and "Don't let old Satan play any more pranks with you," said Guy, to all of which he replied by bowing low, and saying: "Thank you, ladies; thank you gentlemen; take keer of yourselves, and don't forgit to stop here de next time." He watched until, not only their forms were lost sight of, but until the dust which had been disturbed into thick clouds, had settled; then turning toward the house, he began his favorite air:

"O, gib me de wings ob de angels,"

CHAPTER XIII
REV. JOHN JAY DELIVERS HIS MESSAGE

THE Rev. John Jay was not satisfied that he had been true to the older members of his flock. As a watchman he had only faintly blown the trumpet on some points, fearing the consequences.

Now in deep humility of soul, he plead for grace to declare all the counsel of God. If the spirit gave him utterance, need he have fear as to the result? Was it not written, "For as the rain cometh down and the snow from heaven, and returneth not thither, but watereth the earth, and maketh it bring forth and bud, that it may give seed to the sower and bread to the eater; so shall my word be that goeth forth out of my mouth. It shall not return unto me void, but it shall accomplish that which I please, and it shall prosper in the thing whereto I sent it."

Now he would cry aloud and spare not; he would lift up his voice like a trumpet, and show the people their transgressions, and thus deliver his own soul.

With firm steps he ascended the pulpit, that Sabbath morning, and with a heart full of holy resolve. But as his eye fell on the whitened locks and wrinkled faces of many whose years almost trebled his, involuntarily he cried: "Oh Lord God, I am but a child! how can I do this thing?"

We know how quickly human love runs to protect and comfort the little trembling one, so when the cry was heard, there was a tender gathering up into the arms of the Compassionate One, and there came a heavenly calm and holy boldness. There was no sleepers in church that morning, although some questioned whether they were not dreaming, as this youth, hitherto so modest, and unassuming, in authoritative tones pointed out to them their mistakes and the fearful consequences arising from them.

We want men and women to go from house to house, to gather in those who have wandered from God. But whose fault is it that they have wandered? Answer it, ye fathers and mothers. Your judgment is better than the Almighty's.

When the woman was taken in sin, he said: "Martha do I condemn thee! go in peace and sin no more." Didn't He open up heaven just then, even to that sinner? He who 'knew no sin.' But it does not do for us, standing in our strength and wisdom, to say to the weak and erring, to the young and foolish, "We feel for you; our hearts are not too old—we are not too far removed from you by grace, to know what snares surround you. But we will gather about you with loving hearts; we will give you kindly counsel, not sharp reproof; neither will we condemn you.

"How many little ones do you carry to Christ every day, my brother, my sister? Remember He expects you to lift them up by your prayers and efforts, and bear them to Him. He waits with open arms. Whom by kind words and loving deeds, and earnest prayer, have you drawn toward Him? Or whom have you driven from Him, by reproof, fault-finding, and holding yourself aloof? You are afraid the church will be desecrated by the gathering of our young people; they will have such a pleasant, happy time in their weekly meetings, that they will not reverence God's house. Think you, you are more pleasing in His sight, you who turn out of the way the lame and the blind. Ah, it were better never to have been born, than by narrowness of soul, by false reasoning, and warped judgment, to have led astray, or turned aside from God one of these youthful souls. As fathers and mothers, should you not rejoice that your children are among you; that they are improving the gifts bestowed upon them by God, and fitting themselves to fill higher places in the church and the world than you.

"And now, dear friends, fathers and mothers, men and women naming the name of Christ, by His love I beseech you, go out to-day stripped of your prejudices, and your robes of self-righteousness; go out with humility, with yearning, Christ-like love, and say: 'We are all sinners; we need each other's help, and the Saviour has need of all. We will go hand in hand through joy and sorrow, through toil and temptation, up to the gates of the Celestial city, up to the joys at God's right hand.'"

So the Rev. John Jay delivered his soul. So he scattered good seed, leaving the budding, the blooming, the fruit bearing to God.

But it did not all fall on good ground. Some fell by the way-side, and Satan, snatching it up, sowed seeds of discord in its place. So that in a short time it became evident there were two parties in the church. Those who claimed to espouse the Lord's cause, when in reality they were trying to hold the doors of the kingdom of heaven, so that none but those they thought fit should enter, and others, whose watch-word was: "All souls for Christ. Being all things to all men if by any means we may win them to Christ." The former said the Rev. John Jay was intolerant, and a stirrer up of strife; that he was too much of a radical for them, and consequently he must leave. The latter talked to the Lord about it, and determined to stand by His servant. Their numbers were greatly augmented by the young people, who declared if the minister were dismissed not one of them would ever enter the church. So the old and young were brought together sooner, and in a different manner than was anticipated by the young pastor. But the "right" prevailed, and the Rev. John Jay remained. He soon began to miss a number of familiar faces, while at the same time he observed, with great satisfaction, many for whom he had heretofore looked in vain; some of them the young men who had been induced to spend a social evening with him each week in his study, and among them was Guy Gorton.

Upon inquiry he found that brother Smith, as leader of the movement, had decided to worship God in a room of "their own hiring, where there was no young boy to teach them their duty."

As the croakers went out, the young people flocked in, and never did Fourth street church witness such a revival as during that winter. Side by side were found gray-haired parents and their children seeking to learn of Jesus' love, and many a heart that had long resisted all other influence, was led by youthful pleading to forsake sin and turn to Christ. Old and young were secretly drawn together in the bonds of Christian love and sympathy. Even the Association became a family gathering at which the young people did the work and entertained the older folks, they, good, simple souls thinking there never were such talented young men and women, and there never could be such a society as the Association of Fourth street church. "But," they added, "all this and much more, would never have been but for our dear, faithful pastor, the Rev. John Jay."

CHAPTER XIV
"WEEPING MAY ENDURE FOR A NIGHT"

GUY had lost his cheerfulness, his sisters thought. Certainly he had not his old gayety of manner, and they anxiously inquired if he were sick.

"I am sure you must be," urged Ruth; "won't you see a doctor, Guy? Then there is another thing, you read too much; indeed you will injure yourself if you continue to study so."

But he only laughed at their fears, and continued to spend his evenings at home over his books. Seeing that he did not seek other society, the girls gave little entertainments; not costing much to be sure, not more perhaps than some little things they needed, but now did without, so that he might be surrounded by pleasant company, and acquire a taste for the society of good people.

Now it never once occurred to Guy that his sisters were doing this for him. He thought they must be becoming more fond of society, and it pleased him very much, for he did not see why they should not shine in the very highest circles. Before long he meant that they should. And now when their friends came, he did his best to entertain them for their sake, and they were overjoyed at his returns of brilliancy and wit.

Now that the winter had really set in, and promised to be severe, Ruth recollected that Guy's overcoat had not been taken out of the cedar chest, where it had been laid in Spring.

"It is no wonder he has not asked for it," she thought, as she looked at the thread-bare sleeves, and noticed the rusty appearance of the whole coat. Spreading it out, she looked at it, then sitting down thought of what could be done. "Now there is hartshorn, that dissolved in water, cleans cloth beautifully; but even if I did scour it, Guy could never wear a thread-bare coat."

Then came the question: "How can he get another? I know if he could, he would have had it by this time. I must have been thinking of myself and my own clothes, or I should not have lost sight of this so long. I will see how much money there is; at any rate if it should take every cent in the house, Guy must have the coat."

For a long time Ruth sat in the cold room making plans; finally she decided to have a talk with Agnes about it, because it would never do, not to let her have a share in the pleasure of making Guy comfortable. That night the bed-post and rocking-chair were appropriated, and there was a long, earnest talk. Agnes was not so much surprised as her sister anticipated, when she found that Guy was a great way off from making a fortune. For ever since the time Ruth refused to purchase her dress, Agnes had been finding out things she never dreamed of before. It was Ruth who was surprised to find that Agnes knew so much of the real state of affairs. In one way it was a relief, now that she did know, and Ruth felt that a great part of her burden had gone; but it was gone from her to be laid on Agnes, and that thought was more painful than the burden had been.

"It is to be divided equally, remember," said Agnes. "O, I am so glad that I am earning money, Ruth."

Ruth urged that as she was older, she should bear the greater part of the expense; but Agnes would not consent to this; and finally it was settled that each should give half. Then they were perplexed as to the manner of doing it. Agnes thought it best to tell him, and let him order it himself; but Ruth was sure he would not take the money. Three months before, she would not have hesitated to offer it; but he had changed since then, and something told her he had resolved to be less dependent in the future.

"I don't like concealments," urged Agnes; "I felt meanly in acting so about your dress, Ruth."

Ruth smiled, and said: "You always had a tender conscience, child, but there is no other way of doing this, I am convinced."

Agnes yielded to Ruth's judgment, and Martha was sent with the old coat to the tailor, and told to say that Miss Ruth would call in the afternoon.

"When is it to be done?" asked Agnes, eagerly, when Ruth returned.

"On Christmas eve; and only think, Agnes, it will be four dollars less than we supposed. He will make it of the finest cloth too."

"Christmas is coming," said the children many, many times, during the ten days that followed. Ruth's visit to the tailor, and "Christmas is coming," said she and Agnes, as many times as the children. Yes, Christmas was coming, it was drawing near, bringing gladness as it always does; but something else was coming, and drawing still nearer.

The shadow of a great sorrow had fallen. Had they looked in Guy's face they would have seen it; but they were busy with their little presents for each other, and for Martha and Philip. Besides, they rather avoided Guy, for fear he should read their secret. So it grew and grew, until they could escape it no longer. Guy was ill of a fever.

All at once, without a word of complaint, he was taken down, and to all their entreaties that he would speak to them just once, there was no reply.

"O Guy, my brother, my darling, speak," moaned Ruth, as with an agonized voice and look she bent over him. "To think of your lying here alone, suffering through the long night, and no one near to give you even a drink of water."

So she went on talking and bathing his burning brow, while Agnes, giving one earnest look, in which her whole soul seemed to go out, hurried to send Martha for the doctor; then she went back, and putting her arm round Ruth, drew her away.

"Don't take me from him, Agnes; I have the best right here," she cried, fiercely, starting up from the seat into which Agnes had placed her. "I did not help to benefit him; I set him no good example. I must save him now, even if I should die for him."

"Sister Ruth," and her words were slow and measured, "our lives cannot save Guy; only one power can. Look to God, dear sister; he is our only help. And He *will* help us," she added with strong emphasis.

"O, will He, Agnes; are you sure?" and Ruth looked into the face of her sister, waiting for her reply, as if into the face of God.

"He will help us," came again. Then they threw their arms round each other and cried.

"What is it?" asked Agnes, when the doctor shook his head.

"Brain fever, I fear," was the reply.

"Will he die?" almost shrieked Ruth. "You will save him, doctor. O, you won't let Guy die."

"Do you know, my child, you can kill your brother, and you will if you give way to this grief. I will leave no means untried. You are a Christian; you know how to pray; there is greater comfort in that than in any of my assurances; but I give them to you; your brother shall live if it is in the power of man to save him."

Agnes murmured, "O God, give him skill, and give us strength," while hope revived in Ruth's heart, and she listened eagerly to the doctor's directions.

"You will have many days of nursing, it is probable, and you must take it in turn," he said; "but at night it will be well to have a friend. There is a great deal of restlessness then, and one feels lonely. Be sure you give the medicine promptly, and keep up the ice applications, as I shall be back in a few hours."

"Whom can we get?" asked Agnes, when he had gone.

"Don't let us have any one, Agnes; no stranger could take care of Guy, as well as we," said Ruth, beseechingly.

"But, Ruth, if anything should happen, if Guy should grow worse, we would blame ourselves for not doing all the doctor told us."

"Very well, then. You know best, Agnes. I can't think to-day."

Without saying more, Agnes went down stairs, and told Martha to see if Miss Smithers was at home, and if so to tell her to come right away, but not to sew. "Then leave this note with one of the school children," she added.

She met Ruth's scholars as they came, and sent them away quietly, telling them when Miss Ruth was ready she would send them word, and then she tried to take her breakfast. "I must be strong," she said, and tried to eat, but she could not swallow. There was Guy's place, but he was not there. "Will he ever be again!" The question came, but she drove it away. He was in God's hands and so was she. She could take nothing back, but rest in the thought of His fatherly love and compassion.

Miss Smithers came, and Agnes was not mistaken in her. She was ready for every emergency, and never failed to give the right comfort, at the right time. Even Ruth grew to depend upon her, and to miss her kind face when she was compelled to leave them, and seek rest. Agnes had not thought of asking her to give up her work, only to have her stay with them at night. But Miss Smithers did not mean to leave either day or night, until Guy was out of danger, and Agnes gladly yielded the point.

When the sorrow through which the sisters was passing, became known, they had the fullest sympathy of friends. Miss Smithers received all who called, and thus saved them from many painful interviews. For at such times when there are many hearts to feel for us, and to offer the most delicate expressions of sympathy, there are always coarse natures who know no other manner of showing their sympathy than by opening up our wounds and making us bleed afresh.

"How many friends we have, Agnes. I did not know so many cared for us. If Guy recovers we shall be very happy," said Ruth, as Miss Smithers told them of the many who had called.

Guy lay still unconscious, while the fever leaped through his veins, and almost purpled his fair face. Now he was at his books, then again he was pleading; but all the time there was this thought: "I can't rob Ruth, I can't take her money."

"O, if he would not talk so; if he would say anything else but that, I could bear it," she moaned, and then she whispered that "Ruth, his own dear Ruth was there, that he must not talk any more," but still he went on in the same strain.

Poor Agnes was sorely tried. Here was Ruth breaking out in the wildest frenzy, at times, refusing to eat or to leave the bedside; and here the brother, far dearer to her than life, not able to look at her, nor to say that he understood her when she did not yield to his wishes. If he died, he could not know how great her love for him was. And then the subtle tempter came: "If God loved His children He would not cause them thus to suffer. *Your* life has been harder than that of out-breaking sinners." But while Agnes could not reason, thank God she could trust, and reaching out her hand as a little child, she said: "Lead me in the way that is best for me, and do not let me be afraid or discouraged."

Christmas had come and gone, but they would not have known it, had not Guy's coat been sent home according to promise, the day before. They had meant to hide it from Ruth, but she happened to be down stairs at the time it came, and it was kissed and fondled as though it had been Guy himself. Then it was laid away, no one else knew where. She forgot that Agnes had a share in it, forgot everything but that it was Guy's, and he her own darling brother.

Agnes had never asked the doctor any more questions since the day Guy was taken ill. But she wrote down his directions for fear the least thing should be overlooked, and never administered medicine, or rendered him the slightest service, without breathing a prayer that it might lead to his recovery. So the days passed wearily on, and the crisis drew near.

"We must not tell them," said the doctor to Miss Smithers, on the morning of the day. "It will only more completely unsettle Miss Ruth, while the other poor child need have no more laid upon her. If the worst comes, there will be strength given, and anticipated trouble is always the hardest to bear. If you have any influence over Miss Ruth, keep her very quiet, everything depends on that."

Miss Smithers went up to her room, and was there for a long time. When she left it she carried with her something that made her heart strong and her face bright. If you have ever known it you will understand; if not, no words can give you the idea.

The day wore on and still Guy was restless. The doctor came, looked and went away, but there was no outward change. Night closed over them as they sat watching, the two to whom he was the dearest living thing, and another whose heart had been drawn toward him as if he had been her son.

If faith were dependent upon what is seen only, then Miss Smithers might have yielded to the entreaties of Ruth and the imploring looks of Agnes, to let them stay beside Guy, whose unrest was painful in the extreme, for there surely could be no hope here. But she kept them beside her, whispering: "Trust me this once, children;" and in some way they felt that she must be right.

It was near midnight on the last day of the year. What would the New Year bring?

CHAPTER XV
"BUT JOY COMETH IN THE MORNING"

THEY sat, each one busy with her thoughts, so very different, perhaps, and yet in one respect so alike, when suddenly they became conscious of a change. The sisters started, looked quickly at Miss Smithers, and then would have ran to the bedside, but laying a hand on each, she said, with strong emphasis, "If you want your brother to live, you will not move from here."

They looked at her in surprise, then the truth dawned upon them, and turning, they clasped each other's hand and prayed.

Softly Miss Smithers crept toward the bed, and stooping down she scanned the upturned face. As she raised her head she met the searching gaze of Ruth and Agnes. She smiled, then pouring into a spoon a liquid left by the doctor, in case of such a change, she gave it, then turning down the light to the faintest glimmer went back to her seat.

"He sleeps," was all she said, but there was no more needed. They scarcely breathed after that, they sat so still—holding each other's hand until the gray dawn of the New Year's morning broke, and the doctor came.

His quick eye detected the change as soon as he entered. How his face beamed, and how they loved him then. Beckoning to them when he left the room, they followed into the one adjoining.

"Now, girls, there was a hard fight last night," he said, "but the day is ours, or Guy's. What he needs is to have not a finger moved in the room as long as he sleeps. When he wakens you are each to be as calm and fresh as a May morning, or it will set him to thinking and bring back the fever. Now both of you go at once to bed after you take a cup of coffee, and sleep until Miss Smithers calls you; then she will follow your example. Remember on no other condition can your brother recover," he continued, as they plead to stay and see him waken. As he went out he said: "A happy New Year, my children; you have much to thank God for to-day."

O didn't they thank Him! Their hearts were so full of joy and thankfulness that it was a long time before they could forget everything and sleep. It was noon when they awoke, and yet Miss Smithers had not called them. Stealing to the door they looked in; they wanted just one look at Guy, to be sure it was true and not all a dream, and then they went down stairs.

Martha, little woman that she was, was overjoyed at seeing them and knowing Mr. Guy would soon be well.

"You did not get your Christmas present, dear child," said Ruth; "whenever brother Guy wakens you may go up for it; it is in the top drawer of my bureau wrapped up in white paper."

"Miss Agnes gave me two white aprons, all scolloped round," said Martha, with a beaming face.

"You have been a good girl, Martha, we could not have done without you," continued Ruth. "When Mr. Guy is better, we will tell him you helped to make him well."

"Mother said I should be as good as I could, and if you wanted any more help, she would stay all the time, because Miss Agnes was so kind to father," replied the child.

Miss Smithers appeared looking very tired, but cheerful. "Now girls you may go up, he is awake and wants you. But there must not be many words." Ruth took two steps at once in her haste to get up, but she was so out of breath, she had to recover before going in the room, so that both entered together. Guy was awake and knew them; they could scarcely realize it. They kissed him; then each held a thin hand and told him not to speak. When he grew stronger they should have a good, long talk. He smiled faintly and then fell asleep again.

They would have gone away now, but he held their hands in a tight clasp, and so they sat for hours, until he awoke—tired and cramped, yet afraid to move. That night Miss Smithers insisted upon sitting up, and they went to bed in their own room, but not until they had had a long talk.

"This night, two years ago, Agnes, do you remember?" asked Ruth, drawing her chair over to the fire. "You recollect I went to the theatre, and you refused. If Guy had died, I know I should have lost my reason. If it had only been that once, but although I suffered agony then, you know how often I have gone with him since. This came to me all the time of his sickness: 'You mislead your brother, if he is lost you are to blame;' and O, Agnes, you don't know what I suffered! But I promised God if he would only spare Guy, I would lead a new life and never enter such places again. I see my mistake now, we can never 'do evil that good may follow.'"

"And I have been thinking, Ruth, that I have been at fault, in not making direct appeals to Guy, about his soul. I thought it was better to *live* right, so that he might see there was power in religion; but I find that one thing cannot take the place of another. There must be *talking* and *living*, both. And I think we had better talk more about ourselves before Guy; we have shut him out too much from these things, while in everything else we have thought of him."

"If he would only become a Christian, Agnes, how happy we should be. I should not have a single care then."

"He will, Ruth, I feel it; he will be given in answer to prayer and holy living. But we must live so near to God, that we can *claim* this at His hands."

Guy grew stronger. "Who could help it with such care?" he asked. Agnes, who was compelled to go to school now, very often found herself in the midst of a recitation wondering what she could take home, or what she could make for him, when she went home. Ruth gave herself up completely to him. Feeling that as she had hindered, so now she must be a great help to him in every way. She copied and read for him, and would not have hesitated to undertake a case in court, so that it was of benefit to Guy.

Sometimes as she sat with him, the doctor's and druggist's bills came up before her, and almost made her heart stand still, for during all his sickness she had not been earning anything, and they were depending upon Agnes's salary for everything until she could begin to teach again.

She almost despaired of ever being free from anxiety, but looking at Guy her doubts left her. God had spared him to them, and she would trust Him to help them out of their troubles.

Little Philip came every day, now that Guy was able to sit up, and by his odd speeches and persistent attempts at making a picture of Mr. Guy, proved a constant source of amusement, so that Guy looked for him daily, after breakfast.

Ruth several times attempted a conversation with her brother about the things on her mind, but had always failed in the attempt. It came however in this way. She was sewing, and Guy had been reading. Laying down the book and watching his sister for a few minutes, he said: "I have been thinking, Ruth, if all young men had such good sisters as I, how few would go far astray."

"O, Guy," she said, her eyes filling with tears, "I have been anything but a good sister. I thought of it day and night, when you were ill, and it nearly drove me mad."

"What do you mean, Ruth, I don't understand you. What had you to blame yourself for?"

"The great thing, my neglect of duty. I did not hold religion up in its true light. I lowered the standard, and you did not give it proper respect. I wronged you, Guy, and I wronged God and my own soul. I meant to tell you all this, but something kept me back. My inconsistent life came up before me, and I thought I would wait until you had seen a change in me."

"I see it *now*," he replied; "One can see changes more readily in you, than in Agnes."

"Because there is nothing to change in her. Guy, I would give all the world if I had it, to be the trusting Christian our Agnes is. If you had seen her when you were ill, you would have known how wonderful she is. She thought of everybody and everything, but never once despaired or murmured. I think the Lord spared you because of her."

"Why?" he asked in a husky voice.

"Because, she said the other night, we must live such lives that we can *claim* the answer to our prayers; and that is not the kind of a life I have been living. I did not dare to claim anything; I only *begged* to have you spared, and promised to lead a new life."

Guy's thin hands went up to his face and tears ran down his pale cheeks. "Now is the time," thought Ruth, and going over to him she threw her arms round him saying: "I went with you, Guy, dear brother say that you will go with me. Don't let us three be separated any longer."

And this was Ruth, positive, self-possessed, Ruth. She had never refused him anything, and how much she had done for him, he well knew, and at what great sacrifice. He could not refuse her now, so he drew her down, and kissing her, said: "We will go together, Ruth, God helping me."

In a few minutes Agnes came from school, her face beaming, as usual. She looked from Guy to Ruth, then she knew.

"O, Guy, it has come at last?" she exclaimed, laughing and crying at the same time, and in her joy kissing Guy and Ruth, again and again. Then Miss Smithers had to know, and Guy's friend, the Rev. John Jay.

That night they opened their hearts to each other. Guy told them how when Ruth showed her new dress to him, he had seen himself in a new light, and resolved to be their helper in the future instead of what he had so long been.

"And I will be it yet, girls, don't fear," he added. "If you have to pass through some trying days before then do not be discouraged. It shall be seen my sisters have a brother who is not willing to receive love and everything else without a return."

When he was able to go out the coat was brought from its hiding place. It had been laid away with tears, now it was taken out with smiles. Then both sisters helped him on with it, smoothing it here and settling it there, their faces radiant with pleasure. And Guy, in return, gave them what he knew they would rather have than anything else, a fond, brotherly kiss. They walked with him as far as the office, where Ruth had been that morning seeing that Martha had swept and dusted it thoroughly; but all the way there and home, they could not keep their eyes from Guy, he looked so handsome in his new coat. They had seen no one like him all the way along.

Days, weeks and months rolled on, some of them trying enough, as Guy had said. But the spirit of faith and trust nerved them for the struggle, and in the end the clouds rolled away and the sun shone out.

Guy was at last able to fulfill his promise, for he had now entered into partnership with an eminent lawyer. Very proud he was when he made them his first present of new dresses, but prouder still when he was able to dress them "as such sisters deserved to be dressed."

With their prosperity they did not forget their dear old friend Miss Smithers, and many were the tokens of love and gratitude she received.

Both Ruth and Guy claimed an equal right to Philip, and through them he became a pupil of a celebrated artist; while Martha, who was claimed by the entire household, could not pretend to say which she liked best, and all were served with the strength and love of her whole nature.

They sat by the fire one night talking. "I used to think it impossible for lawyers to be good, earnest Christians, Guy," Ruth said.

"And now?" he asked.

"Now I see my mistake, for I know one."

"Thank God for the grace which can keep the soul unspotted in the midst of corruption and temptation," was the reply. "Yes, Ruth, I, too, have found that for every man and every calling there is the same grace, which if brought to bear upon the life and calling, will exalt the meanest and make it honorable. What are you thinking of, Agnes?"

"Of what you have been saying. If God made such a master-piece as man out of clay, He intends that he shall occupy a high ground, morally, I mean, and place it within the reach of all. How glad I am, Guy, that true position is to be found in this attitude of the soul before God, no matter what the social standing is. Then I have been thinking that if we left ourselves in his hands, He would be continually adding gifts and graces, rounding our angles, and bringing out the full symmetry of every part, so that by the beauty of our character we would draw others to Him."

Guy and Ruth exchanged glances, then Ruth said: "Here is one who is all angles. It would take a great deal of rounding to make me symmetrical and attractive."

Guy slowly repeated: "'But we all with open face beholding as in a glass the glory of the Lord, are changed into the same image from glory to glory, even as by the spirit of the Lord.'"